The Golden Owl

Clockwork Calico Book 1

Lana Axe

AxeLord Publications
ISBN-10: 0692643028
ISBN-13: 978-0692643020

Chapter 1

Enhanced. A marvel of the ages. Superior to all other felines. That's how her creator, Lionel Cogg, put it. He named this special cat Calico Cogg. Cali for short. A masterpiece of engineering, a creation of pure beauty. Who could have guessed that a skinny calico from the streets would turn out to be his most marvelous invention to date? As a self-proclaimed Master Tinker, Lionel had spent years dabbling with gears and levers. Though he'd found success with many of his creations, none had given him the pride he'd felt when looking upon Cali. She was truly a masterpiece.

Cali stretched her paws in front of her and arched her back high. Adding a yawn, she allowed her body to shudder, relishing the sensation as her tight muscles stretched. She had slept so well the night before that she'd scarcely moved an inch.

Rays of sun formed a puddle near Cali's favorite cushion on the wide windowsill. The early morning light, interrupted only by the shadowed crossbars on the window, shone down on her, highlighting the golden facets of her fur. Her brass enhancements twinkled in the sunlight, absorbing its warmth. Turning her head, she gave her side a few licks, calming a patch of black and white fur that had become rumpled in the night. Lifting a paw, she gave it a few licks before rubbing it over her face and nose.

The clatter of a small metal dish made her ears turn forward, standing at attention. Breakfast. With a single bound, she hopped from her perch, her stomach rumbling. The metallic implants of her right paw plinked lightly against the floor as she entered the kitchen. Her mouth watered at the sight of small pink shreds in her bowl. This was a special morning indeed. She normally ate well, but it wasn't every day she was given fresh tuna for breakfast.

"Good morning, Cali," Lionel said as he pushed the bowl toward her.

Cali nudged his ankle with her nose, a loud purr vibrating in her throat. Lionel reached down and ran a gentle hand across her fur, adding a few scritchins under her chin for good measure. After brushing herself against his leg in gratitude, she leaned down into the bowl, lapping up pieces of fish and chewing happily. Fresh and flavorful, this was Cali's absolute favorite meal.

Lionel enjoyed a few bites of pastry as Cali ate her meal. This morning the inventor was dressed in his finest: a white shirt with a high collar, black suspenders and bow tie, beige trousers and dark brown boots polished to a high shine. His normally stubbled chin was shaved clean, his graying brown hair combed neat. On his head he wore a black bowler hat, a bronze key tucked into the band. He had to look his best for the exhibition.

The exhibition was presented courtesy of Ticswyk's many Guilds. As an independent tinker, Lionel had nothing to do with these corrupt organizations. They ran more like organized crime than organized labor. Occasionally they warred with each other, escalating to brawls in the streets. He tried to stay out of their way, but refusing to join them naturally put him on their watchlist. But he wouldn't allow them to control him and his work.

Being outside the trade Guilds made finding work difficult at times but easy at others. He could set his own prices and decide which jobs he wanted to take, meanwhile allowing himself plenty of time to work on his own inventions. If he were to join the Machinists or Engineers Guilds, he'd be forced to take work that could be extremely dangerous. Some members came away injured, unable to work again. The Guild Masters didn't care about a worker's well-being.

Not to mention the requirement of paying heavy royalties to the Guild Masters. Low-paying jobs that the Guild coordinated resulted in a meanly sum for the worker since the Guild Masters skimmed sixty percent off the top. Higher-paying work oftentimes meant working for shady characters involved in criminal activity, and required the worker to keep his mouth shut or risk serious punishment. The law looked the other way when it came to the Guilds. Power and gold were their main objectives, not happy and healthy workers.

Even more troubling for Lionel was the fact that his inventions would be credited to the Guild, not to himself. That simply wouldn't do. Lionel liked to let folks know what he'd created. He took pride in his inventions and had no intention of sharing credit for their design.

For the most part, Lionel had been successful. He'd traveled to exhibitions, displaying his latest gadgets and impressing the onlookers. Some of them were even willing to buy. It was a modest living, but it was done on his terms. He'd earned himself a comfortable middle class existence.

There had been a few occasions where the Guild interfered with his work, though. Two years ago, Guild operatives had sabotaged his steam-powered hammer, leaving him with a bruised reputation. The Builders Guild was using the same tool only three months later, proving that someone had stolen his schematics before tampering with the prototype. It had taken this long to invent something else worth exhibiting, and he was delighted to be demonstrating the enhancements he'd made to Cali. Today he would recover his reputation, even in the presence of Guild members.

Cali took her time finishing breakfast before thoroughly saturating her paw with her tongue. Rubbing it vigorously over her mouth, she removed all traces of the meal. Satisfied, she sat back on her haunches and looked up at her friend. Curiously, she cocked her head to the side as she watched him walk away and retrieve something from beneath a blanket. *He can't be serious,* she thought as she realized what he held.

"Now don't give me that look," Lionel said. In his right hand he held a small crate with dozens of holes drilled into each of its four sides. "I have to keep you hidden before the exhibition starts. That way you'll be a surprise." He grinned at the cat, hoping the explanation was acceptable. He knew Cali hated being confined, but it was a necessary evil today.

Lionel set the crate on the ground and let Cali look it over. With suspicion, she scanned every corner of the crate. Making use of her mechanical eye, she checked it for any sign of a flaw, lest she should become trapped or worse, it fail to hold her weight and she tumble to the floor. It appeared sturdy enough, but she still detested being carried in such a manner. Walking on her own four paws was far more dignified.

"Don't you want to hear the crowd ooh and aah when you come out of here?" Lionel asked, tempting her. "Imagine how amazed they'll be when they first see you."

He makes a good point, Cali decided. Nudging his hand, she allowed him to give her a few pets before trotting inside the crate and settling herself in. It wasn't as bad as she expected. There was even room to stretch a bit. *It's actually quite cozy,* she decided, kneading her paws against the thin cushion inside.

"Don't worry, Cali," Lionel said. "You won't be in there long." He scooped up the crate and held it tightly to his side as he stepped out of the apartment. Securing the door behind him, he double-checked the lock and tucked the key back into his hat.

Ticswyk's cobblestone streets bustled with activity, hundreds of citizens making their way to the exhibition. From the holes in the top of her crate, Cali had a clear view of the sky. Balloons of every color dotted the skyline, their baskets heavy with passengers. Travelers came from all around to view the annual exhibition, and rightly so. Inventors from around the world came to show their latest contraptions. Any citizen in attendance could boast to their friends how they had seen it first. Competition for tickets could be fierce.

Though it was proclaimed that all inventors were welcome, the Guilds frequently blacklisted certain individuals from entering their creations. Guild members were, of course, given priority, and only a few independent tinkers from inside and outside the city were allowed to exhibit. Fortunately, Lionel's application had been accepted this year. He had an inkling that the Guilds were interested to see exactly what he had done to his cat. His descriptions on the submission forms were vague, with only scant drawings of his contrivances. Never again, he promised himself, would they be allowed to steal his ideas. If they wanted to enhance a cat of their own, let them figure out their own method. Cali would remain unique.

The shiny tips of Lionel's boots clicked against the cobblestones as he hurried along, still clutching Cali to his side. Hearing hooves behind him, he paused and turned, waving his free hand to the driver. The carriage came to a halt, the driver hopping down to open the door for Lionel and his crate.

Cali pressed her nose to the crate's holes, taking in the strong scent of the horse. She was black and white with a stocky frame, her long tail swishing as she waited for her passengers to board. "Good morning," Cali said to her.

"Morning," the horse replied with a toss of her head. "Fine day to be out and about."

"I'm afraid I'll be inside all day," Cali replied. "There's an exhibition, and I'm the main event." Never modest, Cali knew she would draw a crowd. She was proud of the fact.

"Is that so?" the horse asked. "It's an honor to pull your carriage." She clicked a friendly hoof against the street and whinnied.

"And I thank you for it," Cali replied. Being proud didn't mean she had to be rude. In fact, Cali was considered quite pleasant by the other animals on her street.

Handing a coin to the driver, Lionel climbed inside and placed Cali's crate next to him on the bench. "To Exhibition Center," he told the man.

With a click of the driver's tongue, the horse trotted forward, the carriage rocking as they went. Cali looked up at Lionel through the holes and mewed.

"You want to look out?" he asked. Lifting the crate onto his lap, he pushed it close to the window opening, allowing her to see the world around her. His hand remained on top of the box for safety.

The wind caressed Cali's nose and rippled through her fur, the scent of fresh bread wafting on the breeze. Ladies in ruffled skirts walked arm in arm with gentlemen wearing top hats. Fine dress for a fancy dinner, let alone a morning gathering. The exhibition was truly a big deal. To her surprise, she found herself growing anxious as they neared Exhibition Center. It was one thing to be a celebrity in one's home, but quite another to be displayed to the masses. Small butterflies fluttered in her stomach. Trying her best to bat them away, she put on a brave face and purred.

"That's a good girl," Lionel said, sticking a finger through the crate and scratching her ear.

The carriage came to a halt in front of a massive stone building, gargoyles grinning from its heights. Huge windows of stained glass decorated the front, the lights inside projecting the colors onto the granite sidewalk. Everything about the building spoke of elegance. The Guilds had spared no expense in its construction.

Lionel stepped out, carefully tucking Cali beneath his arm. With a nod to the driver, he stepped toward the glass doors of Exhibition Center.

"Have a fine day!" the horse called as she trotted away.

Cali intended to. All she had to do was stay calm and look pretty. How hard could it be? She was a natural. And she trusted Lionel completely. He would never let harm come to her. After all, he'd rescued her from a life on the streets, scrounging in trash bins for scraps. He'd seen a diamond in the rough, and what a gem she had turned out to be. She wished there were a mirror around so she could admire all the wonderful enhancements he had gifted her. All her nerves fell away, and she meowed her gratitude to the man who carried her. For her dearest friend, she would gladly put herself on display. This would be a show to remember.

Inside was all alight, gas-powered lamps illuminating every corner of the cavernous interior. Rows of tiny orange bulbs were arranged on a high balcony, greeting the entering guests with the words: EXHIBITION CENTER. Hundreds of voices talked over each other, the puffing of steam engines and clanging of metal gears and levers filled the place with so much sound that Cali retreated to the back of her crate. There were far too many noises to discern which were friendly.

Clutching the crate tightly, Lionel made his way through the crowd. It was a slow process, as those in front of him couldn't manage to walk without stopping to peek at a few inventions that were already set up. Though impatient, they would just have to wait. Each exhibit had a scheduled presentation time, and the Guilds saw that it was followed to the letter.

Finally he arrived at his own booth, complete with a small stage and a riser for Cali to stand on. Behind them hung a metal sign, engraved with the words: CALICO COGG, THE CLOCKWORK CAT. Taking a moment to admire the sign, he placed Cali's crate behind the little curtain beneath her riser. Here she would remain concealed until it was time for the demonstration.

Opening the top of the crate, he allowed Cali to sit up. She stretched her arms and legs and gave a content yawn. The sight of the sign above her made her purr with delight. Lionel had crafted the sign himself, making sure it was bright and polished for her debut.

When she started to step out of the crate, Lionel said, "Just a little longer, Cali." Petting the top of her head, he gently helped her back in the crate. "Your show starts in half an hour. Until then, you still have to stay out of sight."

Sitting back on her haunches, Cali twitched her whiskers. That was a long wait, but what else could she do? Until her audience was in place, she would sit here like a good cat and obey. A voice boomed over the loudtalker—a curious device aptly powered by hot air—startling Cali, who pulled her ears backward in response. The speaker welcomed all to the exhibition and ran down a list of presentations that would be taking place each hour. Visitors hurried all around, rushing to their destinations.

Lionel produced a comb from his pocket, and instead of using it on himself, he gently stroked Cali's fur. Always a fan of grooming, Cali lifted her head, allowing him to comb under her chin. Pressing each side of her face into the comb, she made sure the fur was nice and neat. A quick pass over her belly, and she was all set to be shown. Holding up a pocket-size mirror, Lionel allowed her to check her fur for any strands out of place. She studied every inch of herself before meowing her approval.

"Now's your moment," he said, a proud smile on his face.

Chapter 2

Lionel placed his hands behind his back and waited patiently while the spectators assembled around his booth. All walks of life were present, everyone dressing as finely as they could. Those of lower standing were sent to the back, but they were as eager to hear about Cali as the richer folk up front. Children clung to their mothers' skirts, unsure of the strange goings-on at the exhibition. Bouts of applause sounded across the room as a tall grandfather clock heralded the hour. It was time.

Clearing his throat, Lionel drew in a deep breath before starting his speech. "Ladies and gentlemen, I present to you, the one, the only, Clockwork Calico!" With a gesture of his hand, he signaled Cali to show herself.

Delighted to make her appearance, she hopped up onto the platform, her nose held high, whiskers pointing forward. Taking in the scent of the crowd, she was pleased to find so many in attendance. Not all could be seen, but they couldn't escape her keen nose.

"Ooh," many of the attendants vocalized, impressed at the sight before them. Lionel had done well designing his booth. Cali stood directly beneath an overhead lamp that glowed a deep yellow, projecting its light on her brass enhancements. She shone with a brilliance that allowed even those in the back of the crowd to see her.

Children, and a few adults, shoved their way to the front, determined to get a closer look at the fascinating cat. The rest kept their distance, scrutinizing the feline from afar. Cali scanned their faces with her mechanical eye, zooming in and out among the crowd. Mostly smiles, she noted, as the spectators gazed upon her.

One man caught her attention, the brim of his top hat pulled low over his brow. Dark eyes peered beneath the hat, piercing and analyzing every inch of her, a sinister smile on his face. Realizing that he might be trouble, Cali saved his image to memory.

Sitting proudly at attention, she listened with satisfaction as Lionel ran down the list of her implants.

"You see here that Cali has a number of brass implants," the inventor explained. Running a finger along the metal, he said, "Her tail is included of course, augmenting her natural balancing skills. The implant allows her more stabilization and control." He paused a moment to allow the crowd to take in the information.

Cali spun around, waving her grand tail for all to see. One, two, three flicks, and she spun back around, curling her tail around her body. The audience applauded, and she dipped her head in appreciation.

"The implant running along her spine allows for higher flexibility, and it also gives her more strength."

Cali lay down on her pedestal, allowing Lionel to run his hand along her back. With a nod from her designer, she stood and stretched herself low, almost to a pounce position.

"And now, ladies and gentlemen, please direct your attention to Cali's hind legs." Cali turned sideways, allowing the crowd a view of her left hind leg. "These enhancements allow her to jump far higher than the average cat. They also soften the landing when she gets where she's going." He gave a nod that said, *Show them, Cali.*

With pleasure, she indicated with a flick of her tail. In a fluid hop, she dropped from the raised pedestal to the ground, right at the spectators' feet. Many of them stepped back in surprise, some of them gasping at her sudden appearance.

"Note the flexibility of her spine as she jumps down," Lionel said. "And now the power of her legs as she returns to her pedestal."

With those words, Cali leapt, her enhanced legs carrying her from the floor, past the stage, and up to the top of her pedestal. The audience erupted in applause.

"A full ten feet from a standstill!" Lionel announced, adding some applause of his own. "The average housecat can jump only about five feet without running." A wide grin spread across his face. "Now, who'd like to see Cali run?" He rubbed his hands together in anticipation.

The children in the crowd squealed their excitement, and the men and women cheered. Everyone was eager to see what else Cali could do.

Feeding off their excitement, Cali made herself ready. Jumping from her pedestal, she landed once again at their feet. The crowd parted allowing her the freedom to run. Taking the opening, she bolted past the crowd, sprinting toward the nearest wall. Instead of stopping, she leapt and turned midair, her hind legs bouncing from the stone wall and feeding her momentum. In less than a second, she was back among the crowd, but she didn't stop there. Once again she leapt, this time flying high in the air. With a twist of her enhanced spine she somersaulted above her pedestal and brought her feet back beneath her. Landing softly on her perch, she raised a paw and bowed to the audience.

"Bravo!" the men cried. The ladies followed suit, crying "Encore!" The children laughed and squealed, delighted by the phenomenal cat's showmanship.

"There's more to her than that!" Lionel announced, eliciting more applause. "She has enhanced claws on her right paw, making her a deadly foe to mice." This was one selling point that Lionel considered adding to other cats. It would improve the skills of mousers everywhere.

Cali raised her right paw, which appeared almost ordinary at first. When she unsheathed the claws, the audience jumped back in surprise. They weren't prepared for the razor-sharp knives Cali displayed. Though very small, they were terribly sharp and deadly to mice. Cali turned her wrist left and right, allowing the light to hit her enhanced claws. After a moment, the crowd moved forward again, the spectators eager to examine this miniature weapon.

"Don't worry," Lionel reassured them. "Cali is in full control of her claws, and no human will be harmed. I can't say as much for mice, though." He gave a quiet laugh, and many in the crowd echoed him. "Of course, Cali could use these for defense as well, should she be attacked by a large rat or some other vicious creature."

Cali almost grimaced, but caught herself. She didn't like the sound of that. It was best to be on the offensive rather than the defensive, but Lionel was correct. The claws could be used in either case. She could extend or retract them as easily as her true claws on her left paw.

Lionel held up a small sheet of paper and presented it before the crowd. "A demonstration," he said.

Cali swiped her paw at the paper, shredding it in four neat strips. Generous applause followed. Before the crowd quieted down, Lionel tossed the paper into the air, and Cali pounced after it. Slicing her claws through the air, she struck the paper repeatedly. As she landed on her platform, a shower of confetti rained down on the crowd. The children raised their hands, hoping to catch a piece or two, giggling with delight. The women laughed and brushed the paper away from their hair, the men applauding before removing their hats to brush the paper bits away.

"And finally," Lionel said, "we've come to Cali's mechanical eye implant. I'm sure the large purple lens hasn't escaped anyone's notice. Don't worry, Cali's true eye remains intact. I've only added to it and given her the ability to see far better than the average cat. With this eye, she is able to magnify her target, seeing it more clearly. She can also detect heat signatures, meaning no mouse can escape her. Cali will always know where it's hiding."

Cali tilted her head left and right, allowing the light to dance off the implant. The spectators looked her over, wondering what it must be like to possess such an enhancement. Most of the children brought their fingers to their eyes, their mothers stopping them before they could hurt themselves. Cali would have laughed, but this was a serious moment.

"Now, you might ask," Lionel began, "how do these implants work? What is their power source?" Cali spun on her pedestal. "You'll see she has no outward gears or windup mechanisms. Cali is powered on the inside, by a system of tiny gears. Her power source is her own beating heart."

The crowd gasped, instantly shocked.

"That's correct!" he went on. "Cali's own heart and blood vessels are incorporated into the enhancements. She cannot wind down, nor does she require any special rest." With a glance at Cali, he added, "Well, no more than any other cat."

Polite laughter came from the audience. Most of them knew how much cats enjoyed their rest. From his pocket, Lionel drew out a small device, no bigger than the average pocket timepiece.

"This device allows me to alert Cali if she's away, calling her back home." When he pressed the button, a tiny red light illuminated on the tip of Cali's tail. If she were away, she would know that Lionel needed her to return home, most likely for her dinner.

"If I could have complete silence for one moment, those in the front row might be able to hear the soft ticking sound associated with Cali's gears."

Cali bounced down to the edge of the stage, a hush falling over the crowd. Everyone in the front row leaned in close, some cupping their hands to their ears.

"I hear it!" a boy shouted.

"Yes, yes—I hear it too!" a man announced. Others joined in, agreeing that they could indeed hear the ticking of Cali's clockwork components, though they were no louder than a whisper.

"You see, ladies and gentlemen," Lionel said. "Cali is far from the ordinary cat. She is one-of-a-kind, a true masterpiece of modern engineering. Some of these enhancements will be available for your own mouser, should any of you wish to discuss the matter." He would never make a cat quite like Cali, but he would be happy to add certain features to other cats for the right price. Many areas of Ticswyk were plagued with mice and rat infestations, and he could certainly make a difference to the community while still making a tidy profit for himself and Cali.

Turning to Cali, Lionel said, "How about one more run for the children?"

With a nod of her head, Cali obliged, leaping from her pedestal and dashing across the room. Twisting and turning, she leapt through the air torpedo-style, much to the delight of the children. Not only did they laugh and point, they clapped their little hands as fast as they could. The adults applauded as well, elated to see the charming Cali repeat her best stunt. She was a marvel. Far more interesting than machines and gears, she was a living, thinking being, made spectacular by the hand of man. She was what this age of industry was all about.

With the first show complete, many of the spectators lined up to converse with Lionel. Some had simple questions about Cali, while others were eager to employ him to enhance their cats. One woman even asked if Lionel could possibly enhance her bird. Unfortunately, the implants would be too heavy to allow her parakeet to fly. Ground birds might be possible, though. The woman went away disappointed.

The sinister looking man in the top hat took a very close look at Cali, spending several minutes listening to her ticking. Keeping a polite, soft posture, she surveyed him as well, giving him a thorough going-over with her mechanical eye. When he pulled out a watch to check the time, she could clearly read his name on the inscription: JAMISON MORCROFT.

The name nearly made her shudder, but she managed to keep her composure. She knew him from Lionel's conversations with his sister. Morcroft was a member of the Engineers Guild, serving as its second in command. He was a dangerous man, notorious for his criminal behavior. He once hired a crew to tunnel beneath Ticswyk's museum of art in order to steal a painting the curator had refused to sell him. Not only did he steal that particular work of art, he got away with several antiquities as well. Among them was an Egyptian statuette of pure gold, which he quickly melted down to hide the evidence. Three guards were injured during the heist, but Morcroft didn't care. Neither did he face punishment. The Guild stepped in, and the law backed down. Rumor had it that the judge assigned to the case found himself quite wealthy all of a sudden, and he retired to a warmer climate.

After putting his watch away, Morcroft approached Cali and stared for another minute. She did not back away, though the fur on her back ruffled slightly at his nearness. Thankfully, he did not reach out to touch her. The urge to strike out at him might have been too strong for her to control.

Finally he walked away, and Cali relaxed. Lionel, having finished his conversations, approached Cali and scratched under her chin. She lifted her head and purred, enjoying the attention. From his shirt pocket, he retrieved a small tin, the sweet-smelling treasures inside making Cali's nose tremble. Liver! Lionel offered up a liver treat, which Cali gobbled readily. With a soft mew, she begged for a second and was quickly rewarded with another treat.

"Only two more shows to go," he said, patting her head.

The second show went the same as the first. Cali performed her tricks with pride, and Lionel's confidence soared, his voice becoming more and more inspired. They made a great team, putting on a show the crowds would never forget.

Morcroft attended the second show as well, keeping himself well out of view in the back. But nothing escaped Cali's superior eye. She watched him closely, scrutinizing his every move without missing a beat in her performance.

After the second performance, Cali was given yet another liver treat. A child ran up as she was swallowing, and pressed his little face as close to hers as he could. Lifting his lollipop to his mouth, he narrowly missed depositing sugar on her fur.

"Not so close now," Lionel said, wagging a finger at the boy. His mother stood close by, oblivious to the boy's actions.

The boy backed a few inches away, but lifted his hand and poked his chubby fingers at Cali's rear leg implants. Cali remained calm and patient. When the boy cocked his head to the side, she could almost hear the wheels turning in his head. He was up to no good.

Reaching a sticky hand toward her tail, he curled his fingers around it. Lionel reacted with lightning speed, batting the child's hand away. The mother reacted with shock, grabbing her son and holding him to her side.

"Forgive me, ma'am," Lionel said convincingly. "You see her tail is electric, and if the boy had tugged on it, it would have given him a nasty shock. It could have knocked him clear out the door and across the street!"

The woman gasped, her eyes growing wide. "You leave that cat alone!" she scolded, grabbing her son by the arm. She stormed off, child in tow, heading straight for the exit.

Lionel laughed and stroked Cali's fur. Amused, Cali flicked her tail and nuzzled her head in his hand. After a few licks to smooth her fur, she was ready for the final show of the day.

More onlookers gathered, the biggest crowd yet as the sun was beginning its descent. Morcroft was among them, still pulling his hat low in an effort to hide himself. When Lionel squinted out in the crowd and gave a disapproving grunt, Cali knew he had seen him as well. Why he had attended all three shows was a mystery, but both Cali and Lionel knew that he was plotting something.

The show went well, Cali performing at full energy despite the late hour. By now Lionel had perfected his act, throwing in a short encore for the final crowd. They closed to thunderous applause. A few spectators threw roses onto the stage, many of which Cali caught in her teeth, taking a bow after each one. She enjoyed showing off, and the crowd appreciated it as well. Soon the applause ended, and the crowds departed for home.

Silence descended over Exhibition Center. The machines were shut down, and no announcer called out shows and times. Lionel opened the crate and asked Cali to step inside once more.

"There could be people hanging around for an extra glimpse," Lionel explained. "I wouldn't want anyone to bother you."

Cali knew he was referring to Morcroft more than any other. He was a dangerous man who had taken an interest in Cali, and Lionel was crating her only to protect her. Without argument, Cali hopped inside and settled herself into the crate.

"Attagirl," Lionel said.

To Cali's delight, the carriage that drove them home was pulled by the same black-and-white horse as before. "Good evening," Cali said to her. "I don't think I caught your name before."

"I'm called Nellie," the horse replied. "And you?"

"Cali," she stated.

"How was the exhibition?" Nellie asked.

"Fantastic," Cali replied. "I enjoyed every moment."

The horse stopped in front of Lionel and Cali's apartment. "Glad to hear it," the horse replied. "I had a fine day as well. Lots of carrots and plenty of sunshine."

"Wonderful," Cali said as she was taken out of the carriage. "I hope I see you again, Nellie."

"Likewise." The horse tossed her head and whinnied before trotting off into the night.

Nestled inside her crate, Cali waited for Lionel to carry her inside. Securing the door first, he opened the crate and scratched at her ear.

"We did real good today, Cali," he said. "You were a sight to behold." Lifting her, he hugged her close to his heart.

Cali purred softly, enjoying the warmth as he held her. Back on her feet, she waited patiently as he poured a saucer of cream, which she lapped up readily. After kicking off his shoes, Lionel sat himself in his favorite chair, which also happened to be his second-favorite invention, and pressed the lever that allowed him to recline. Cali jumped in his lap and curled herself into a ball. The day's events played over in her mind as she drifted off to sleep. Her dreams echoed with praise and applause, a content smile lingering on her face.

Chapter 3

Cali awoke bright and early the next morning, still snuggled on Lionel's lap. All the excitement of the exhibition had come to a close, leaving both of them exhausted and grateful for a good night's sleep. Lionel was still fast asleep, his head rolled to one side, his arm hanging off the side of the recliner. Cali sat up and meowed.

Lionel didn't wake.

Her tummy beginning to rumble, Cali tried again. No reply. Leaning up on her hind legs, she pressed her cold nose to his cheek. He awoke with a start. She mewed softly and snuggled her head against his face.

"All right," he said, grasping the lever to bring the chair back upright. With his feet on the floor, he pulled himself up. "Wouldn't want to be late to breakfast," he said.

Cali hopped off the chair and raced toward the kitchen. As Lionel fidgeted with a tin can, she weaved herself between his ankles, purring all the while. After what felt like an eternity, Lionel placed a metal dish on the floor, the aroma of its contents flooding her nose. Shredded beef! Cali plunged into her breakfast and lapped up every bit, barely taking the time to taste it.

Lionel laughed as he watched her eat, twirling his finger around her tail. When she had finished, he took the dish and cleaned it before preparing his own meal. A wedge of cheese and a soft hunk of bread sounded about right. He took a seat at the table with Cali perched at his feet.

"You'd think I never feed you," he said, offering her a bit of the cheese.

She took it gratefully and savored it on her tongue.

The sun's rays filled the apartment, bringing with it a warmth that usually made Cali sleepy. Instead, she was surprised to find herself energized this morning, the previous day's strenuous activities having no ill effect on her. No soreness, no fatigue; she felt like a spry kitten.

A knock at the door alerted them both, and Lionel moved to answer it with Cali, as always, at his feet. When he opened the door, he smiled, happy to see who had come calling. It was his sister, Florence.

Florence stepped inside with a nod to her brother and a pat on the head for Cali. She stood only an inch shorter than Lionel, her honey-colored hair piled on top of her head, a small yellow hat sitting on top of her curls. She wore a ruffled yellow dress and high-heeled leather boots, an outfit suited to her position as factory overseer. The gas lamps produced by her workers were the very same that lit the streets of Ticswyk. She was a busy woman, but she always made time for her brother.

In fact, Lionel saw his sister almost daily. With his apartment attached to the factory, it was natural that the two would come in contact regularly. Lionel was frequently employed by his sister as an engineer, responsible for the repair of several of the factory's machines. He was a far more dependable worker than a Guild member, and his presence kept her from relying on corrupt Guild leaders. Though the machines did not break often, Florence knew she could count on Lionel when they did. His expertise with all things mechanical, and his hardworking nature, made him a model employee.

Plus, she enjoyed having her brother around. In exchange for his work, she paid him a small stipend and allowed him use of the apartment rent-free. He was perfectly happy with the arrangement. An ample workshop came along with the deal, and he was able to use scrap parts produced by the factory in his own tinkering.

Cali helped at the factory as well. When she wasn't busy sitting on her windowsill, observing the world, she served as head mouser for the entire building. Being a lamp factory, the place was not overrun with vermin as a food-producing facility might be. But the mice still got in, and Cali was happy to dispatch them for Florence and her workers. In exchange, she received numerous pets and loads of praise from the workers, as well as small bits from their lunch. It was perfect payment.

Occasionally, Cali would leave a fresh-caught mouse in Lionel's shoe as a gift. After all, it was about the best thing a cat could give her dearest friend. He would feign his delight and praise her, but she knew he wasn't keeping the mice. He'd toss them out in the refuse bin when he thought she wasn't looking. Cali didn't mind. Even she got tired of the taste on occasion.

"Morning, Florence," Lionel said. "You want some breakfast?"

"Actually," she said, producing a small bundle from her basket. "I brought these."

Wrapped in brown paper, Cali recognized immediately what was inside the bag. Pastries! Florence opened the parcel, confirming what Cali already knew. A half-dozen assorted pastries awaited inside, some filled with red jelly, some with creamed sugar. Cali loved the cream-filled pastries best of all. Twirling her tail around Florence's legs, she hoped to be given a bite.

Florence did not disappoint. Pinching off a portion of the pastry, she dipped it in the cream before passing it to Cali. Purring with delight, Cali lay on the floor, licking at her prize. It was the perfect dessert to complement the breakfast she'd already eaten.

Lionel chose one filled with jelly and took a few bites. "Mmm," he said as he chewed. "I'll get you some tea." He hurried into the kitchen area, where a pot of water was piping hot on the stove, a soft whistle alerting him to its readiness. Returning with two cups of tea, he sat down at the table.

Florence did likewise, nibbling on a bit of pastry and sipping at her tea. "How was the exhibition?" she asked.

"Oh, it was marvelous," Lionel replied, wiping the jelly away from his mouth and licking his fingers. "Cali was spectacular. The crowd loved her."

Smiling, Florence replied, "I wish I could have been there."

"I'll tell you who I wish hadn't been there," Lionel said. "Jamison Morcroft."

Shaking her head, she asked, "Why was he there?"

"Stalking me, I suppose," he replied with a shrug. "He came to all three shows. Looked Cali up and down and sideways," he added. "Mark my words, he'll try to replicate my invention." The tinker's eyes sparkled, and he giggled quietly. "He won't succeed."

Pursing her lips, Florence replied, "He doesn't have the soft touch for such work."

"That's exactly right," Lionel agreed. "And he doesn't have the patience. Cali's enhancements were delicate work. I pity any poor creature Morcroft experiments with."

"Maybe the Guilds will keep him in check," Florence offered.

"Pfft," Lionel replied, waving his hand. "They'll let him do as he pleases. Heck, they may not know that he's up to anything. But I'll keep an eye out. I won't have him harming any animals. If I can do anything to stop him, I will."

"Just be careful," she cautioned. "Morcroft is a dangerous man. I think he'd do more harm to a person than an animal."

"You might be right about that," he replied. "Still, I'm going to let the police know to keep a close eye on Morcroft's workshop." The police were not run by the Guilds, but they often backed down where Guild members were involved. And some of them could be bribed to look the other way. Still, there were many officers Lionel trusted. They were a good lot who tried to do right by the law in spite of the Guilds.

Finishing her pastry, Florence wiped her hands and dabbed a handkerchief to the corners of her mouth. "The boiler's gone out on the conveyor again. I had to move Adelaide off it. I know it's her fault, but I thought she'd learned her lesson last time."

"I can fix it this morning," Lionel said. With a grin, he added, "Just don't let Adelaide near it afterward."

"You have my word on that," Florence said, laughing. Taking a final drink of her tea, she stood and brushed at her long yellow skirt. "I guess I better get over there," she said. She gave Lionel a kiss on the cheek before turning toward the door.

Her brother shuffled along behind her, opening the door and bidding her good day. As she left, he spotted the daily newspaper waiting on his doorstep. "Hoo hoo!" he called as he saw the front page. Bringing the paper inside, he said, "Look here, Cali! We made the front page."

Cali didn't move closer, instead adjusting her mechanical eye to see it from a distance. There she was, photographed in black-and-white, proudly seated on her pedestal. Pictured next to her were two less-interesting inventions: a steam-powered engine for a horseless carriage, and a contraption made of magnets that supposedly heated food. They were nothing compared to Cali. Her only regret was the lack of color in the photo.

"Exhibition Center's finest inventions," Lionel read aloud. "You made the list, Cali." Setting the paper aside, he said, "I better get over to the factory before the shift starts. I don't want them getting behind." He disappeared into the washroom to make himself presentable. After donning a fresh set of clothes, he put on his hat and headed for the door. "I almost forgot," he said. Trotting back to the kitchen, he retrieved a small tin. "Dried fish," he said, placing the tin on Cali's windowsill. "Now don't eat it all at once," he told her. "Save a bit for later. I might be a while fixing that machine." He stroked Cali's fur and scratched under her chin before taking his leave.

With a full belly and ego, Cali plopped herself in the sun puddle spilling over her cushion. The warmth overwhelmed her, and her eyelids grew heavy. Before she knew it, she was fast asleep.

* * * * *

"That should do it," Lionel said as he tightened the last bolt. It had taken nearly three hours of work, but the boiler was working once again, and production could continue.

41

"That's wonderful news," Florence said. She handed him a few coins and two paper bills for his work.

"That's too much," he said. When it came to his sister, Lionel had a tendency to undervalue his work.

"It's the same as I'd pay any other engineer," she replied. There would be no argument, nor would he try to give back the money. She'd paid a fair wage, and he would accept it, like it or not.

Tucking the money into his pocket, he said, "Thanks, Florence. Let me know if you need anything else."

"You know I will," she said with a smile. In a swirl of her skirt, she headed out onto the production floor.

Lionel cleared away his tools, tucking them neatly into a leather holder. One wrench hadn't been cared for properly and had nearly rusted through. He found out the hard way when he tried to use it and it snapped neatly in half. It was time to find a replacement. There were a few other supplies he needed for his workshop, so he decided to make the trip across town to his favorite smithy. An old friend of his ran the forge and made some of the finest tools Lionel owned. He always gave a fair deal and a fine product, far better than items produced in a factory.

A light drizzle of rain fell from the sky as Lionel stepped out onto the sidewalk. The cobblestones glistened with wetness, the city's guttering systems doing a decent job of draining most of the puddles. Never one to remember an umbrella, he pushed his hat down on his head and proceeded despite the rain.

Three blocks away he checked for a carriage, but there were none to be found. The rain wasn't letting up, and he was quickly becoming chilled. One more block and he knew of an alleyway that would serve as a fine shortcut. Overhangs on the buildings on either side would block most of the rain and give him a chance to warm up.

The streets were empty as he crossed, the sky growing ever darker. He proceeded down the alleyway, happy to be out of the rain. A door opened behind him, but he took no notice. The only sounds he heard were his own footsteps and the rain pelting the roofs above him. Catching him unaware, a set of hands reached out for him, and a burlap sack was forced over his head. Lionel struggled and kicked, but the hands were far too strong.

Lionel began to shout, "Let me go!"

"Quiet," a voice grumbled.

Lionel shouted again, earning him a blow to the stomach. He doubled over, the breath escaping his lungs. A second set of hands grasped his feet, the first not letting go of his arms. Together the thugs strung him between them, carrying him off to places unknown.

No matter how hard Lionel tried to keep his bearings, he lost track as they moved along the alleyways. Twice they flipped him upside down, laughing at his predicament. He kicked and squirmed, but it was no use. It only resulted in tiring him and angering his captors. Several minutes passed, and he knew they'd gone at least five blocks. They turned again, circling, he suspected, to throw him off-guard. It didn't matter. Lionel had no idea where they were.

Finally, a heavy door opened, its metallic joints creaking from the effort. Lionel was plopped onto a chair, the sack still covering his head. The two men made short work of tying him to the chair, the thick ropes squeezing his chest and arms. His feet were also bound, preventing him from running away. One man finally lifted the sack slightly to place an oily-smelling gag in Lionel's mouth. Crying out was no longer an option, not that it had done him any good. It had already earned him a beating, and he wasn't about to ask for another.

The two strong men walked heavily away from him, their footsteps disappearing with the clang of a door. Lionel was alone. Behind him somewhere he heard the whirring of machines. They puffed and vibrated, but he smelled no burning fuel. For all he knew, they were in the next room. It was impossible to tell what the machines were for or which building he'd been brought to.

A clock ticked somewhere to his left, but he couldn't be sure of the time. It was less than an hour since he'd left the factory, of that he was sure. No one would miss him yet, and that meant no one was coming to help.

His mind turned to his beloved Cali, and how she might worry that he was so long away. She was a good cat, and he didn't want any harm to come to her. Someone might have kidnapped him in order to get to her. His worst fear was that someone might try to take her apart in an effort to duplicate the technology. The thought sent a chill down his spine. He tried to convince himself that this situation had nothing to do with her. Florence would look after Cali, and she would be fine. It was that thought alone that kept him from panicking.

Minute after minute, Lionel listened to the ticking of the clock. He began to count the ticks, attempting to keep track of how long he'd been tied up. Not that it mattered. Whoever had done this had a plan, and he had no choice but to sit and wait until someone cared to share it with him.

After twenty minutes to Lionel's count, a different door opened. This one was not nearly as heavy when it closed again. Footsteps tapped along the hardwood floor, a third tap the sound of a gentleman's cane. Lionel knew whoever it was, he was no gentleman.

"Lionel Cogg," a voice said, followed by a deep, throaty laugh.

Fingers lifted the burlap sack, removing it from Lionel's head. At last Lionel could see who was responsible for his mistreatment. Jamison Morcroft stood before him.

Chapter 4

Cali napped away the morning. When she finally awoke, the sun had disappeared, leaving her cushion in the shadows. The smell of dried fish flakes on her windowsill set her stomach to rumbling, and she helped herself to a few mouthfuls. Licking her paws clean, she looked out the window. The clouds had gathered while she slept, dousing Ticswyk with rain. She was glad to be indoors.

Hopping from her perch, she padded toward the kitchen. Lapping up some water from her dish, she contemplated what to do next. Lionel was still away. His scent lingered in the apartment, but it was not fresh. She searched the apartment for her favorite ball of yarn, finding it tucked away behind Lionel's chair. She batted it for several minutes before losing interest and returning to her window.

An hour passed and then another as she observed the world from her perch. Carriages and horses trotted along the cobblestone road, and a few citizens hurried along, hidden beneath their umbrellas. Two pigeons sat across from her on a neighboring roof, their feathers masterfully shedding the rain. She wondered what they might be talking about for so long before they finally flew away. Sleep overcame her once again.

It was dark before Cali awoke, her stomach reminding her that she'd missed her dinner. The apartment was dark, but Cali's keen eyes needed no light. She moved expertly through the apartment, wondering if Lionel had returned. Still her nose could not track him. He hadn't yet returned home.

There were many possibilities that could keep Lionel away. He might have needed special parts for the machine he was working on, or he was needed for some other task around the factory. He could have been called away on urgent business, or he was invited to dine somewhere. None of those, however, would have kept him from his duty to feed Cali. The tin of fish was empty. It hadn't been enough to last all day.

He was diligent and methodical, always returning home at a reasonable hour. The height of the moon let Cali know it was late, far later than her friend would normally stay out. *I suppose I shouldn't worry,* she said to herself. After all, Lionel was a responsible adult, even if he didn't have her superior feline qualities. He could look after himself.

Cali could look after herself as well. She was hungry, and there was likely a mouse or two in the factory next door. Through a small flap in the apartment's rear door, Cali let herself out. This door did not lead into the street. It led straight onto the factory floor, where a cat could tend to her duties as mouser.

Inside the factory was dark except for a few gas lamps which hung from the ceiling. With no light at all, the factory's security system would not work. It was one of Lionel's designs, though several such contraptions had been invented in recent years. It was a set of six egg-shaped brass fixtures with lenses attached. They were orange in color and worked similarly to Cali's mechanical eye. They were programmed to detect human shapes moving through the factory. Anyone walking through here while the system was armed would set off alarm bells that could be heard for several blocks. Cali's ears were grateful that her feline form would not trigger the alarm.

She had heard tales of other security systems, some far more sophisticated than Lionel's design. His served its purpose, though. Theft at a gas lamp factory was rare since it offered little worth taking. Florence kept the strongbox in a hefty safe right underneath one of the orange-eyed fixtures. It would take ten men to carry the safe away and a load of dynamite to blast the door. No doubt, the money was quite safe. Other than that, only a few strands of precious metal could be found, and a person would have to know an awful lot about the construction of lamps to find it. By screening her workers carefully, Florence avoided the possibility of someone sharing that knowledge.

Scanning the perimeter with her eye, Cali checked for any sign of movement near the floor. There was no kitchen or cabinets full of food, so rodents had a better chance of finding a bite to eat on the ground. The workers often snacked while they worked, as most were unwilling to halt production for a lunch break. Florence didn't mind, and she was quite happy to pay them for the extra time worked.

Cali appreciated it too. Whenever she visited in the daytime, the ladies would share whatever they were eating. If not for them, Cali would have missed out on a world of flavors. Peanut butter, powdered cheese, and brioche were among her favorite forbidden snacks. Lionel would never feed her such things. He considered them junk. But the factory ladies were all too happy to treat her.

Occasionally, Cali would choose a lap to sit in, making it impossible for the chosen worker to complete her work. Temporarily relieved of her duties, the worker would stroke Cali's tricolored coat and listen to her soft purr. That was until Florence came to see why production had come to a halt. Then she would shoo Cali away, insisting she return to the apartment. Florence was all business at the factory, but she was kind enough when not at work.

On silent paws, Cali crossed the factory floor. Rows of workbenches stood idle, wiped clean after a day's work. Her eye scanned beneath them, searching for anything that might whet a mouse's appetite. Nothing.

The area had been swept—not a speck of dust remained behind.

Moving along, she passed the conveyor belts and made her way to the boiler where Lionel had been working that day. It still held his scent, and she wondered if he had returned home since she had gone out. A high-pitched squeak sounded from the shadows, her ears standing at attention. Swiveling them right and left, she homed in on the source. Slowly she turned to face her prey, a blue-gray mouse approximately twenty yards away.

There was little cover for stealth in this area, so Cali skirted along the boiler and crept between rows of tables, hiding herself behind their wooden legs. The mouse was oblivious. He sat near a chair in the glass polishing area, holding a small crumb in his paws. His teeth worked at the treat, his nose and whiskers twitching.

Cali's stomach rumbled, and she stopped in her tracks for fear the mouse might hear it. She was soon moving again, her mouth watering in anticipation. Closing in on her prey, she lowered her posture, her tail jutting straight behind her. With a wiggle of her haunches, she activated the implants in her back legs. Armed with the strength of three cats, she leapt. Flying a little higher than she had planned, she gave the mouse time to see her. He turned and ran. The chase was on.

Dashing through the factory, hot on the mouse's heels, Cali could almost taste him. Manipulating her implants, she adjusted her stride to that of her prey, ensuring she would not overrun him again. The mouse was hers. His tiny legs carried him surprisingly fast, his will to live strong. In an unsuspected twist, the mouse stopped dead in his tracks, sending Cali flying past him. As she spun around to continue the chase, he darted beneath Florence's desk.

"You're trapped now," Cali called to him. "Come out and I'll make this quick." Swiping her enhanced claws beneath the desk, she pulled out a large wad of dust and fuzz. Tossing it aside, she swiped with her long tail, its brass implant scraping against the wood. When she felt nothing, she peered beneath the desk, her pupil widening in surprise. The mouse was gone! Yowling in anger, she checked again, this time with her mechanical eye. A faint trail of heat left behind by the panicked mouse led inside the desk. A small hole had been chewed through the bottom, leading inside a drawer.

Grasping the handle, Cali pulled the drawer open and hopped inside. The frantic scratching of rodent feet scraped against the drawer above. The mouse had an escape plan. As Cali jumped from the bottom drawer, she spotted the mouse as he emerged from the top center of the desk, running as fast as his legs could go.

"Clever!" she shouted, giving chase.

In blind flight, the little mouse dashed through the factory, searching desperately for cover. His eyes landed on a blackened piece of machinery with a pipe leading all the way to the ceiling. Racing toward it, he found himself only one pounce in front of the calico. Leaping with all his might, he grasped at the pipe, hoping to climb to safety. To his horror, the metal was too slick, and he slid back to the ground.

"Got you!" Cali cried as her paw landed on the mouse's tail, pinning him to the floor. "You gave me quite a chase," she told him. Licking her lips, she prepared herself for the single bite needed to end the mouse's existence.

"Wait!" the mouse squeaked, barely able to catch his breath. "Don't eat me yet! I have information for you. It's about your friend."

Cali cocked her head to the side. "Friend?" she asked. Did he mean Lionel? What could this little mouse possibly know?

"Yes," the mouse replied. He stared up at the cat, her purple eye large and intimidating. Shuddering, he focused his gaze to her normal green eye, which was far less terrifying. The clang of her metallic enhancements as she had chased him left no doubt in his mind. She was the strangest—and scariest—cat he had ever encountered. He panted a few times before saying, "Promise you won't eat me after I tell you."

Weighing her options, Cali decided she could quite easily catch another mouse. This one had given her more of a chase than most. "Agreed," she said. "But your information had better be valid, or I take it back."

"Fair enough," the mouse replied. "You're the strange calico that lives with Florence's brother, right?"

"Strange?" Cali repeated, slightly insulted. "I do live with Lionel, yes."

"He was kidnapped," the mouse said.

"What?" Cali asked, stunned. "When? Why?" Narrowing her eye, she demanded, "Tell me everything you know."

"I will, but could you please let go of my tail?" the mouse asked, looking down at his tail.

Cali moved her paw away and waited patiently. If the mouse tried to run, she would have his hide.

"Thank you," the mouse said. "And my name is Emmit. I believe you're Cali, correct?"

She nodded.

"Well, Cali, I saw your master this afternoon," the mouse began.

"He's my friend," she corrected. "Cats have no masters."

"Of course," Emmit replied. "I was having a snack a few blocks away near the bakery," he explained. "I heard a shout and ran to see what was happening. Sometimes humans shout when they've dropped food, so it was worth a look."

Cali rolled her eyes. *Mice,* she thought with disdain.

"I didn't see any food," Emmit went on, "but I did recognize Lionel. He'd been here earlier in the day, so his face was fresh in my mind. Two large men stuck a bag over his head and carried him off."

Cali couldn't believe her ears. "I have to find him," she said. She started to turn away, but the mouse stopped her.

"I know where he is," Emmit said. "I can take you to him."

Cautious of accepting the mouse's help, she asked, "Why would you do that?"

"Because you didn't eat me," Emmit replied. "I am grateful for that. You can also be of help to me in the future."

"How so?" she asked impatiently.

"Promise never to eat me when I'm prowling this factory. That's all I ask."

"You have my word," she replied. "Now take me to Lionel."

With a squeak, the mouse bounded across the factory floor, leading her to the rear exit. A tiny crack in the bricks allowed the mouse to squeeze his sleek body through to the other side. But there was no opening for Cali. Determined to follow, Cali leapt for the door handle and tugged, pressing her hind legs to the wall next to the door. It popped open a few inches, and she hopped through it before it banged closed behind her.

"Good job," the mouse said. Without waiting for a reply, he scurried along the cobblestones. He led her to a drain in the street and said, "It's faster if we go this way."

Looking at him with disgust, she asked, "How much faster?"

"At least fifteen minutes," he replied.

With a groan of displeasure, Cali followed Emmit down into the sewer tunnels beneath the street. The stink assaulted her nostrils immediately, making her wish she could shut off her sense of smell. A rat looked up from across a river of brownish-green liquid, the look on his face one of amazement. A cat and mouse walking together was a sight to be seen. Cali flicked her tail at him and continued on.

When they emerged through another tunnel, Cali desperately yearned for a bath. She fought the urge, telling herself it would have to wait until Lionel was safe. She had been careful not to touch anything, so she probably didn't smell as bad as she feared. Unfortunately, her nose still burned from the stench, and it would probably be days before her sense of smell returned to normal.

"This way," Emmit called, his voice now a whisper. He didn't want to alert any humans to his presence, for fear they would chase him away. His deal with Cali was far too precious to lose.

The night was still and damp. The rain had finally retreated, though the clouds remained. Gas lamps lit every street, projecting a warm glow and a gentle hum. Cali found them familiar and comforting, despite the pounding of her heart. Her mind reeled with the knowledge that someone had taken Lionel. If he were hurt, she would see that the person responsible was throttled. She would do it with her own paws if she had to.

They rounded a corner, and Emmit announced, "It's not far now."

A narrow alleyway lay before them, but it was plenty wide for a cat. She slinked low, her fur bristling with anxiety. A scent came to her nose, faint at first, but strong enough to make it past the memory of the sewers. It was Lionel's scent. Her pace quickened, her four paws moving silently over the cobblestones.

"In here," Emmit said, leading her to a door.

The metal door was sealed tight without a single crack wide enough for a mouse to squeeze through, let alone a cat. Its only visible weakness was a small, rectangular window about two thirds of the way up.

"Do you know of a way in?" Cali asked.

Emmit shook his head. "You'll have to wait for someone to open the door or claw your way through it."

"I will if he's in there," Cali pledged. Crouching low, she leapt high, aided by her enhanced legs. Her metallic claws gripped the edge of the window, allowing her to dangle momentarily. There, slumped over in a chair, was Lionel. Her heart sank at seeing him in such a sorry state. He had obviously been mistreated, and anger boiled in her belly. She had to get to him. He would do no less for her.

Allowing herself to slide back to the ground, she made ready for another pounce. Determination gleamed in her eyes. "I'm going in!"

Chapter 5

Launching herself on powerful haunches, Cali slammed into the window. It was no use. She didn't weigh enough to bust through it. Another leap, and she slashed at the glass with her enhanced claws, leaving behind scratches but little else. "I need something heavier!" she shouted to Emmit. She was getting in one way or another.

The mouse looked all around, but there was nothing at hand to use as a tool. "We could run along the street until we find a brick," he offered. Though he wouldn't be able to lift it. That job would have to fall on Cali.

Peering through the keyhole with her mechanical eye, Cali zoomed in on her friend. The noise from her fight with the door had caught his attention, but he looked more frightened than relieved. From this distance, he probably couldn't tell who was at the door. His sight was not as advanced as Cali's. *He should have put some implants on himself,* she said to herself. *Then he would be strong enough to break free.*

Observing her closely, the mouse formed an idea. "What about your claws, Cali?" he suggested.

"They're not strong enough to break the glass!" she replied. "You saw me try." Was he not paying attention?

"No, I mean you could pick the lock and open the door," Emmit suggested. It could be done far quicker than running up and down the streets looking for something to throw.

Looking at her claws, she said, "I've never picked a lock before." Jamming a claw into the keyhole, she pulled and tugged, trying to rip the lock mechanism apart.

Emmit cleared his throat. "If I may?" he offered. Climbing onto her tail, he ran along her back and onto her outstretched paw. Taking control of her claw with his tiny paws, he worked at the lock. "It takes a bit of finesse," he explained. "Brute force probably won't work. These locks are made of reinforced steel."

Making note of his fine movements, Cali activated all her senses. Every nuance was worth remembering if she was to learn Emmit's technique. Next time, she wouldn't need his help. At least, that was her intention as she memorized the delicate procedure.

"Have you done a lot of this?" Cali asked, narrowing her eyes. She wondered if her new companion might be some sort of criminal. But who was she to judge? The life of a street mouse was far different from her own.

"On occasion," Emmit replied, still concentrating on the lock. "I've never used a claw, though. A hat pin makes a fine lock pick."

The lock released with an audible click, music to Cali's ears. "Nice work, Emmit," Cali said. "You're one handy mouse." She licked his face with her scratchy tongue.

Emmit cringed a little, unused to such treatment from a cat. With little effort, the clockwork cat leapt for the door handle, pressing against it with her hind legs. It opened only an inch, forcing her to swing sideways. With her feet now against the door's edge, she gave a strong kick. Despite its weight, the door opened a few more inches, allowing her to enter.

Emmit darted in behind her. Though his part of the bargain was fulfilled, he didn't want to leave Cali now. This place was obviously dangerous, and she might need more of his help. With her friend in danger, she might not think as clearly as she should. Emmit, being a level-headed mouse, knew his presence might be crucial. He would stay and see things through.

Despite her instinct to run to her friend, Cali slowed her pace and crept into the room. The lights were dimmed, a single lamp shining on a workbench near Lionel. Turning to Emmit, she placed a claw to her lips, urging him to keep quiet. The mouse understood. Scanning the room with her mechanical eye, she looked for any sign of a security system. Something mounted to the wall reminded her of the egg-shaped cameras at the factory. Standing perfectly still, she waited to see if it was moving. It wasn't. If it were armed, there would be an indicator light, but there was none. Feeling a bit safer, she crept forward.

Lionel stirred momentarily in his chair but slumped back to his defeated posture. He had no idea Cali was approaching. A quiet click sounded from a corner of the room, and Cali's ears twitched in response. Zooming in with her eye, she spotted the source of the noise. A shining bit of round metal had clanged against the steel bars of a cage. She nearly gasped as she realized what the metal was. It was a tag, attached to the collar of a guard dog. Locked safely in a crate was a large black-and-tan dog, his pointed ears standing at attention. His long nose sniffed the air.

Swallowing hard, Cali wondered if the dog knew she was there. For a moment she debated whether it was safe to keep moving, but there was no other choice. She had to get to Lionel, even if the dog could bark and alert its master. Switching her vision settings, she scanned the crate for its lock mechanism. It was secure. Unfortunately, a thin wire extended from it, snaking its way across the room. If she ran into it, the dog would be set loose. *Clever,* she thought. Most intruders wouldn't notice the wire before finding themselves face to face with the dog.

"Psst," she whispered to Emmit.

The little mouse padded to her side. Pointing with her paw, she directed his attention to the dog. Emmit's eyes grew wide.

Silently she mouthed the words "trip wire" and traced its outline with her claw.

Emmit understood. He was too small to set it off just by walking, but if he tried to jump up to Lionel or the workbench, he might brush against it, allowing the dog to run free. He wouldn't last long in its powerful jaws. He would have to step carefully.

Moving low to the ground, Cali proceeded with caution. Lionel wasn't far. A sudden movement to her right startled her, and she looked in time to see the dog, baring his white teeth. A low growl rumbled in his throat, and Cali's fur bristled in response. Hopping over the trip wire, she found herself at Lionel's side.

In a single pounce, she landed on his lap. He jolted upright, surprise written all over his weary face. He mumbled something inaudible through the gag in his mouth. Taking great care with her claws, she slashed at the fabric.

"Cali!" Lionel said. "How on earth did you find me?"

The calico let out a soft mew and hopped down from his lap. With three swipes of her claws, she freed him from the ropes that bound him. Bringing his wrists around to the front, he rubbed them each in turn.

"Thank you, Cali," he said. "I don't know how you managed it, but I'm ever so glad to see you." Lifting her off her feet, he cradled her in his arms.

When she returned to the ground, she placed herself between him and the trip wire. She hoped if she didn't budge, he would step over her, thus avoiding the trap. With a loud meow, she encouraged him to leave quickly.

The meowing caught the dog's attention, and a warning bark rang out. Lionel looked over at the dog and scoffed.

"He's caged," he assured her. "Don't you worry about him." Turning his attention to the workbench, he began moving items around. "Now what did that Morcroft do with my tools?" he asked, scratching his head. He spotted them beneath another bundle and pulled them free. A soft plink sounded from beneath the workbench, and he wrinkled his brow.

Cali's body went rigid, fearing a trap had been triggered. With a glance at the dog, she reassured herself he had not been released. But her sigh of relief came too soon. Her delicate ears picked up a soft sound, like a metal ball rolling through a wooden shaft. One look at Lionel assured her that he was hearing it too.

"We better get out of here," he said. Scooping Cali up, he tucked her under his arm. Before she could protest, his foot hit the trip wire, the door to the dog's crate lifting open.

With a snarl and a growl, the dog charged forward, his feet sliding on the wooden floor. Once he gained his footing, he was moving far too fast for Lionel to outrun. Cali had to act quickly. Wriggling herself free of his grasp, she charged toward the dog.

"Cali! No!" Lionel shouted. He watched in horror, fearing she would be killed. To his amazement, she pounced with a yowl and a hiss. Landing square on the dog's back, she tore at him with her claws. The dog let out a loud yelp of pain. He spun, faster and faster, trying to shake the cat from his back. She held on tight, but a vicious shake of the dog's body threw her to the ground. Lionel ran to her aid.

A loud crack signaled that the rolling ball had found its target. A bang and a sizzle followed, the pair holding their breath and waiting. It was too dangerous to move, but staying put could be deadly. A soft whistle began at the opposite end of the room, growing louder as it moved near. Cali's eye could see tiny holes opening in the wall. With a paw against Lionel's face, she turned his head so he could see too.

"Stay low!" he cried. Clutching her and shoving her beneath him, he laid flat on the floor. Two dozen tiny arrows sped past, plinking against the wall. "We've got to get out of here!" he cried, scrambling back to his feet. "Morcroft's booby-trapped the whole place!"

The dog licked at his scratch wounds a few times before bounding toward them again. Cali hissed and arched her back, but Lionel grabbed her anyway. Holding her tight against his chest, he sprinted for the door. The dog was on his heels in two strides. He grabbed onto Lionel's pant leg, tugging furiously.

"Let go, mongrel!" Lionel shouted as he tried to pull his leg free.

Emmit, who had stayed well out of harm's way, suddenly sprang to action. He set his sights on a large paper bag only a few feet from the crate. Immediately he recognized the scent of dog kibble. Its unmistakable aroma had drawn his attention shortly after they'd entered the room. If he could get the dog focused on food, his companions might be able to escape.

Racing across the cold floor, Emmit flung himself on top of the bag. Pulling and tugging with all his might, he tried desperately to rip it open. He failed. Using his teeth, he bit and gnawed, but the paper was too thick and would take several minutes to chew through. *They won't last that long,* he told himself, frantic. Thinking on the fly, he spotted the dog's dish only a hop away. Jumping down, he grabbed the bowl and banged it against the metal crate.

The dog's ears perked up, but he didn't let go of his prey. When Emmit banged the bowl against the kibble bag, the dog couldn't resist the familiar rattling. With a high-pitched bark, he released Lionel's pant leg and made a mad dash for the kibble. Emmit raced out of the dog's path, heading for his companions. Meanwhile the dog slashed into the bag, sending chunks flying all over.

Twisting the door handle, Lionel cursed. It wouldn't budge. He kicked it hard, but only managed to make his foot throb. Rushing back to the workbench, Cali in tow, he dug through the pile of tools. Beneath them was a small pouch filled with dark powder. "This'll do!" he said, racing back to the door.

Emmit stood clear, watching with interest as Lionel sprinkled the powder on the floor. Producing a small box of matches from his pocket, he lit one and took a few steps back. Holding Cali tight, he tossed the match toward the powder.

A loud bang echoed throughout the workshop, rattling the mouse's bones and nearly knocking him off his feet. When the smoke cleared, he saw Lionel's shape stepping through the open door. As the mouse ran through behind him, he glanced at what had been the door. It was now bent and scorched.

Lionel tried to get his bearings, not knowing exactly where he was. Cali struggled against him, wanting to be put down. Too afraid she might get lost, Lionel clutched her tighter and stroked her fur. She ceased her wriggling and relaxed in his arms rather than force him to release her. Struggling too hard could harm her old friend.

"We'll just have to find us a carriage," he said. When he saw the empty streets and all the lamps lit, he knew the hour was far too late. No carriages were in service. "We'll find our way," he said, reassuring both Cali and himself. He walked a few blocks before he realized where he was. "Ah!" he said. "It's this way." With new confidence to his steps, he hurried along the sidewalk.

A few blocks from home, he remembered that his hat had fallen when he was kidnapped. His apartment key was tucked inside it. If he wanted to go home without waking his sister for the spare, he needed to retrieve the key. Taking a deep breath, he found the courage to return to the alley where he'd been attacked. It was dark, and his hat was black, making it nearly impossible to find.

"Drat," he said, swiping at the darkness with his foot.

Out of nowhere, he saw a glint. It was the key! And it was moving. Wrinkling his brow, he watched as the key approached, still attached to his hat. It came to a halt at his feet, and he bent down to retrieve it. He heard a mouse squeak as he lifted it, and he jumped backward. So did the mouse. Emmit ran and flattened himself against the wall to avoid Lionel's feet. Humans had heavy feet, and frightening one could result in a mouse being crushed.

"Um, thanks," Lionel said to the darkness. He wondered if he was dreaming or if a mouse had really just brought him his hat. Placing the hat on his head, he spun on a heel and headed for home.

Chapter 6

Carefully securing the door behind him, Lionel

checked it two more times before setting Cali down. She looked up at him, examining him for any sign of injury. He was walking fine, though he had a few bruises. All in all, he seemed to be all right.

Making his way into the kitchen, Lionel's mind was still whirling from his harrowing day. He grabbed a tin from the cabinet and opened it, dumping the entire contents into a bowl. He placed it on the floor for Cali. Taking a seat cross-legged on the floor, he stroked her soft fur as she ate.

"I'm glad you found me, Cali," he said. "I don't know how I would have got out of there. You're the best cat in the world." Leaning in, he kissed the calico on top of her head. No implant could have taught her to come to his aid. There was no invention that could install empathy or loyalty into a cat, or a person for that matter. Cali had learned all that on her own. She was even more remarkable than he ever thought possible. "Until the day I die, Cali, I promise to be the best friend a cat ever had."

A purr rattling in her throat, Cali nudged his hand and returned to her meal of sliced chicken and gravy. It was superb, and she licked every drop from her dish before washing the remnants from her face.

Lionel was more at ease after he'd had a while to sit and think. Before turning in for the night, he shoved half the apartment's furniture against the front door. The rear door was secure enough. If Morcroft wanted in that way, he'd have to make it past the factory's security system, and Cali could hear a pin drop, even if she were asleep. "Let's have a little rest," he said to her. She happily followed him to the bed and curled up near his feet.

* * * * *

"Lionel? Are you in there?" Florence called from outside the door. It wasn't like him not to answer after the first knock. She began to wonder if he'd gone out early.

Cali kneaded her paws against Lionel's chest, gently rousing him from his sleep. With a soft mew, she let him know it was time to get up.

"Morning already?" he asked. Sitting up and grabbing his pocket watch, he saw that it was actually midmorning. He'd overslept, but the rest was necessary. Hearing a voice at the door, he said, "Florence." Tossing the covers aside, he hurried to the door.

"There you are," Florence said as he opened the door. "Are you ill? You don't look so good."

His disheveled hair wasn't the only sign something was amiss. He wore only one sock and his pant leg was rolled halfway up. "It was a rough day yesterday," he said. "And then a rough night too."

"What happened?" she asked, concerned.

"Have a seat, and I'll tell you," he said. Retrieving an upholstered chair from the front door, he motioned for her to sit.

"Redecorating?" she asked, taking note of the piled furniture.

"Not at all," he replied, sinking into a chair of his own. "I was kidnapped after I left the factory yesterday."

Florence gasped and pressed a hand against her heart. Cali hopped onto her lap and purred, calming her. "By who?" she asked, scratching at the cat's cheeks.

"Jamison Morcroft," he answered. "He's got some scheme he's working on, and he wanted me to help him. I refused."

"That's why he kidnapped you?" she wondered.

"He sent his henchmen to rough me up a little," he said, his face reddening with anger. "Nothing too bad since he didn't want them caving my head in." Pausing, he worried at the purple bruises on his wrists. "Left me with a bag over my head until Morcroft returned making his demands."

"At least he let you go," she commented.

"He didn't," Lionel said. "I don't know how long he would have held me there. It was Cali who came to my recue."

Florence gasped again and looked down at the cat in her lap. "How on earth?" she asked.

"Beats me," Lionel replied. "But there's no doubting that she's one amazing cat."

"Do you know what Morcroft is planning?" she asked. "Something criminal?"

"No doubt it's criminal," he replied. "But I didn't get the details. He said he'd pay me, but I'd have to join the Guild. That way he could keep a close eye on me."

"You have to go to the police," she said.

"I can't do that," he replied. "I don't have any proof, so Morcroft can't be punished. What he can do is want revenge for my squealing, and I can't have that. He could harm you or Cali to get back at me."

"Then what are you going to do?" she asked.

"Lie low for a while," he replied. "And fashion a better lock for that door. Maybe I'll rig up a device to let me watch my own back while I'm out."

Nodding, Florence said, "Those are good ideas."

"I think he's got some scheme in mind that has to do with Cali," he went on. "After seeing him at the exhibition, I should have known he'd try something." Shaking his head, he said, "I thought he might try to steal Cali. I never dreamed he'd come after me."

"Did he ask you about her?" Florence asked.

"He mentioned that whatever he's making could use technology like hers," he responded. "He's interested, make no mistake. But I was careful. Her creation is a trade secret, and he won't pry it from my lips. I burned all her schematics as I implemented them. All that information is stored in the safest place I can put it." He pointed to the side of his head. "Let's see him steal the design from in there."

With a sympathetic smile, Florence said, "I'm glad you weren't hurt."

The ideas were already forming in his mind as he stared over at the front door. "I know just what to do with that door," he said. "Morcroft's henchmen won't be getting through it in a hurry. If they manage it, they'll wish they hadn't."

Florence smiled. "That's the brother I know," she said. "Morcroft isn't half the inventor you are."

"I'll need to take the train to Woodsborough," Lionel said. "It's the quickest way, but they don't allow cats on board. Can you keep an eye on Cali for a few days?"

"Of course," she replied. "What's in Woodsborough?"

"An old friend of mine," he said. "He makes the parts I'll be needing for the new lock mechanism. And he won't breathe a word of it to any living soul."

"I'm glad there's someone you can trust," she commented.

"What about you?" he asked, suddenly growing concerned.

"Of course you can trust me!" she replied. What was he thinking?

"Not that," he said. "I know I can trust you. I meant, are you going to be safe while I'm away? Not to mention Cali. Morcroft might even try something at the factory."

"The factory has its security system," she reminded him. "I know the installer," she said with a wink, "and it works perfectly well. I'll look in on Cali and make sure she's fed. I can take care of us both." A patch of lace on her skirt covered a hidden pocket. Reaching inside, Florence pulled out a small revolver, just enough so her brother could see it.

Raising his eyebrows, he nodded his approval. She'd always had an independent nature, even as a child. Their mother used to say "that girl is plumb wild." Florence lived life on her own terms, uninhibited by society's rules. She didn't need a husband to protect her. She could make her own way in life, and that's exactly what she did. Lionel was proud of his sister. She was strong and intelligent, and she wasn't afraid to let others know it.

"I'll leave right away," he said. "And I'll be back as quick as I can. The train runs through Woodsborough daily, so it won't be long."

"Do you need funds?" she offered.

He groaned a bit, reluctant to ask for money. The truth was, he had very little of it at the moment. Most of his earnings went into whatever invention he was working on. One invention paid for the next, and any extra he spent on treats for Cali. He was never good at saving money. Scratching at his head, he muttered, "I'm not sure how much everything will cost…"

As he trailed off, Florence opened her cloth purse and pulled out a stack of neatly folded bills. "Here," she said, taking several from the bundle. "Use what you need, and bring the rest back."

With a nod of gratitude, Lionel took the money and secured it in his vest pocket. "Thank you," he said, feeling a little embarrassed. He was the one who should be taking care of her, but the smile on her face let him know she was proud to take care of him instead. He'd work it off in the factory soon enough.

Observing his own manner of dress, Lionel said, "I guess I should get cleaned up before I go."

"I quite agree," she said, laughing. "Looking like that they'll think you a vagrant and send you away from the station."

Lionel laughed too and rose from his seat. Embracing his sister, he said, "I'll see you soon."

Cali hopped from Florence's lap and watched as she exited to the factory. Weaving between Lionel's ankles, she let him know she would miss him while he was away.

"I'm glad that Morcroft didn't try to steal you," he said. "I'd have his hide." Lifting the calico, he cradled her in his arms. "If he ever does come near you, you use every skill you possess to get away from him. Don't hesitate for one second to use those claws."

Nuzzling his face, she purred near his ear to let him know she understood. She didn't fear Morcroft. Only the thought of losing her dearest friend could frighten her. For her own safety, she held no fear. Like Florence, Cali could take care of herself. As a kitten on the streets, she had learned how to fight and how to survive. Life with Lionel was comfortable, but she hadn't forgotten her origins.

After a quick bath and a change of clothes, Lionel was nearly ready to depart. All that remained was to put out plenty of food for Cali. After filling two bowls, he brought a few tins out of the cabinet and left them on the table so Florence didn't have to go looking for them. Patting Cali on the head, he said, "Florence will be around to keep the bowls full." She purred back at him and followed as he made his way to the door. After securing his hat, he exited through the factory door, leaving most of the apartment's furniture propped against the main entrance. Cali perched herself on her windowsill and watched him as he climbed into a carriage and disappeared from sight. There was little else for her to do but nap.

After a few hours snoozing, Cali wondered if she shouldn't check in with Florence at the factory. Stretching her back and legs, she started to hop down, but movement outside the window stopped her. Standing on his hind legs and peering inside the window was Emmit.

"Emmit," she said, happy to see him. "Come inside."

The blue-gray mouse squeezed himself through the window. "Good day, Cali," he said.

"I'm glad to see you weren't hurt," she said. "You didn't come back with us last night, and I was a little worried." In a short time, she'd grown quite fond of the little mouse. It would be a shame if he came to harm. He was now among the few she considered her friends, and that meant he would have her protection whenever he needed it.

"I spotted a pastry wrapped in newspaper," the mouse said. "I couldn't pass that up. After I ate, I was too tired to follow. But I'm here now." He grinned at her with tiny white teeth.

"I wanted to thank you for all your help last night," she said. "I might never have found Lionel without you. I'm in your debt."

"I'm glad I could help," Emmit replied.

"And great work with that dog!" she said, remembering how heroic the little mouse had been. He hadn't hesitated for a moment, even though he could have been eaten in a single gulp. "You were brilliant."

"Ah, go on," he said, tilting his head to look modest. In fact, he was quite proud of himself. "There was nothing to it, really," he said, waving his hand.

"When you think about it, dogs are easy to manipulate."

"I think you're one extraordinary mouse," she said, purring. With her scratchy tongue, she licked the mouse's fur until every inch of him was clean and soggy.

Emmit cringed with each stroke, unused to such attention from a cat. Her breath smelled faintly of chicken, and he was pleased that it lingered on his fur. The scent of food was far more pleasing to a mouse than the flowery scents humans often wore.

When she was finished, she curled up next to the mouse. Settling in, the two enjoyed a brief nap in the sunlight. A rumbling tummy woke Cali, and she hopped from her perch. Emmit followed.

"There's plenty of chicken if you'd like some," she said.

"I'd be delighted," the mouse replied, licking his lips.

Cali watched astonished as the little mouse gulped down the food. For such a small creature, he could certainly eat a lot.

"Where's Lionel?" Emmit asked as he licked his fingers. "Did he make a report with the police?"

Shaking her head, Cali said, "He went off to get parts for the door. He's making the lock stronger and staying away from Morcroft. He said going to the police would only cause more trouble."

"He might be right about that," Emmit said. "What are you going to do?" He didn't know Cali well, but he knew enough to suspect she wouldn't let the matter drop. Her friend had been mistreated, and Cali would find a way to hold Morcroft accountable.

"I want to keep an eye on Morcroft and find out what it is he's planning," Cali said. "He wanted Lionel to work for him, and I'd like to know exactly what kind of work it was. Lionel suspected it was illegal. Maybe if I can figure out his plans, I'll be able to expose him for the criminal he is. Would you be willing to help me?"

Emmit thought about it for a moment. "I'll tell you what," he said. "If you can leave out a bit of cheese for me now and then, I'll swing by Morcroft's workshop daily to check for anything unusual."

"You've got a deal," Cali said.

Chapter 7

With Lionel away, Cali's first instinct was to guard the apartment. Luckily, Emmit could keep his eyes on the streets and let her know if Morcroft was making any sort of move. But there was one other who might see something, and Cali would have to go out to speak with her. It would likely be a while until Florence returned to check on her, so now was as good a time as any.

Undoing the lever that held the window closed, she parted the two sections and slipped outside. Carefully she prowled along the cobblestone street, her eyes scanning each carriage as it passed by. Four went by, but none of them were drawn by Nellie. Sitting back on her haunches, Cali decided to wait.

After nearly an hour, she wanted nothing more than to curl up and go to sleep. But she couldn't leave herself exposed that long, and returning to the apartment without talking to the horse was unacceptable. Grumbling, she pounced across the street and crept along the alleyway. Two blocks away, she spotted another carriage. It pulled over, letting a passenger out and, by sheer luck, it waited for the passenger to return.

Sending power to her haunches, she raced along the street, a black swish of horsetail ahead of her. Rounding the carriage, she meowed with delight. It was Nellie.

"Hello there!" Cali called to her.

"Well, hello!" Nellie replied. "Nice to see you again."

"And you as well," the cat said. "I wanted to ask a favor of you, if you would be so kind." Obviously the horse owed her no such courtesy, but she seemed friendly and helpful. Cali was sure she'd agree.

"What do you need?" Nellie asked, tilting her head sideways. "Need a ride?" She wasn't sure how else she could be of help to such a special cat.

"No, it's not that," Cali responded. "Do you happen to know Jamison Morcroft?"

The horse's eyes shifted from side to side as she thought about it. "Yes," she replied. "His workshop is a few blocks away. He hires us now and again, but he never tips the driver." She shook her black-and-white head.

"That doesn't surprise me," Cali said. "He's an awful man. He kidnapped my friend Lionel and tried to force him to work on some criminal venture."

"That's terrible!" Nellie exclaimed. "Is Lionel all right? He's a kind man. I'd hate to see him come to harm."

"Yes, he's all right," the cat said. "But I fear he's still in more danger. I'm not sure what Morcroft is planning, but if you see or hear anything unusual, would you tell me about it?"

"Of course I will," Nellie said. "We start working just after dawn, and we're frequently parked two blocks south of your apartment. You can meet me there, and if I've seen anything, you'll be the first to know."

"Wonderful," Cali said. "You have my thanks."

"I'm happy to help," the horse replied. Neighing, she bobbed her head at the calico cat.

Cali purred and nodded. It was good to have someone so familiar with the streets keeping a lookout. She'd be able to give perfect directions to wherever Cali needed to investigate. At least it might spare her from navigating the sewers with Emmit.

As the two said their goodbyes, the passenger returned to the carriage, and Nellie trotted away. Cali waved with her tail and hurried back to the apartment. Letting herself in through the window, she scanned the interior for any sign someone had been there in her absence. Everything was as it should be. Curling herself into a ball, she napped away the afternoon.

* * * * *

Emmit padded along the alley, keeping his tiny body near the wall. It was the best way to remain unseen, especially when it came to humans. They had a tendency to shriek or stomp when they saw him.

In an effort to keep his promise to Cali, Emmit had spoken with every mouse, rat, and squirrel he'd come across since morning. None of them had witnessed anything strange. He would ask again in a day or two.

Ducking inside a sewer grate, the little mouse navigated the subterranean like an expert. He avoided every hazard: water, debris, and especially the alligator who hid under Second Street. By now he was quite comfortable with the route to Morcroft's workshop. He'd been traveling there for weeks without knowing what sort of man he was. Now that he knew him to be dangerous, he would take extra precautions. A mouse could never be too careful. An easy meal near Morcroft's place was likely to conceal a trap.

Streetwise Emmit knew the look of most mouse-killing devices. Snap traps were all the same, and he recognized them easily. Sticky traps were a bit trickier. They tended to blend in. He avoided those by keeping his feet clear of all paper, instead skirting around the edge until he was sure it was safe. Tossing a pebble to see if it stuck was also a good idea.

Once, Emmit had seen a small cage trap attached to a spring. It was bated with a juicy piece of sausage. His mouth had watered, and his eyes had gleamed, but he couldn't find a way around the trap. Eventually a fox came along and grabbed the sausage. Being far too big for the tiny cage, it had simply landed on its wide back and bounced off to the side.

Slits of daylight revealed the exit just ahead, and the mouse poked his head out to see if the coast was clear. A few people stood nearby, but they were facing the other direction and far more interested in their own affairs. Staying low to the ground, he continued on his way to the workshop.

Arriving at the door, he stood on his hind legs and looked it over. It was boarded up with several wide planks reaching across it. It would take a lot of work to force it open unless, of course, someone had the use of gunpowder. Emmit smiled to himself. The door was far beyond repair. Morcroft would have to purchase a new one. *Maybe he'll think twice before kidnaping anyone else,* Emmit thought.

For a moment he considered letting himself in through a slit in the planks where the window had been. There could be valuable information inside. Unfortunately, the dog would still be in there too, and Emmit didn't have another trick up his sleeve. If the dog was loose, Emmit might not make it very far before he was attacked. For now, at least, he decided not to take the risk. If there had been anything useful,

Lionel probably would have spotted it. *I'll wait until I see something suspicious,* he decided.

Emmit went about his day and spent the evening close to the workshop. He awoke only a block away, and decided to check on Morcroft before grabbing breakfast. To his surprise, there were three men working on the door. Two were holding the heavy door in place, the third positioning a set of gears. Using a noisy tool, he fashioned the gears to a fixture against the metal, securing them in place. Another large section went on top, forming what Emmit supposed was a security device. It looked impenetrable.

This finding was significant, he decided. If he and Cali needed to get back in, this lock wouldn't easily be picked. He was used to simple locks with tumblers. This one was unlike anything he'd seen. Not wanting to leave before he had all the information, he waited and watched. The men went inside, a whirring noise echoing from within the shop. It was an hour or more before they came back outside. Attaching a thin set of wires to the apparatus, they ran the lines back inside.

That's trouble, Emmit thought. He'd seen a similar device installed at the museum after Morcroft's heist. Basically it let off a charge if the proper key was not inserted into the lock. Anyone who tried to enter uninvited would be blown to bits. The next time they needed inside the shop, they'd have to find another way. Emmit decided to visit with Cali and let her know about the new door.

A few steps toward Cali's, and Emmit's stomach begged for food. A short detour wouldn't waste too much of his time. Stopping near a bakery, he searched the perimeter for a crust of bread. *Jackpot,* he thought as his eyes landed on a half-eaten honey roll. Leaping for it, he covered it with his body and looked all around to make sure there were no competitors watching. Darting around a corner he found a nice opening in the brick to hide in. Nibbling at the bread, he savored its sweet flavor.

With his hunger satisfied, he carried the remaining roll away for safekeeping. Halfway to the factory, he spotted movement. A round metal automaton, barely larger than himself, clinked along on seven legs. The eighth leg held a shiny round object. This was certainly something worth noting. Securing his honey roll in his teeth, he tiptoed toward it.

Oblivious to his presence, it moved along, its steps uneven and clumsy. Closer now, he could see it with more detail. It was all metal, likely brass, and it was scratched and dented on its dome-shaped top. Scrap metal had probably been used in its construction given its shabby state. As it clinked along, Emmit thought it reminded him of a spider. *That's exactly it,* he realized. Someone had built a mechanical spider and set it loose in the streets. But why?

Emmit kept the spider in his vision until it disappeared around the corner of a building. A door opened in front of him, forcing him to a halt, lest he be squished by two humans coming out of the building. Impatiently, he waited for them to step aside before racing after the spider. When he rounded the corner, it was gone. His shoulders drooped as he realized he'd lost it.

With a sigh, he turned around, ready to head back to the factory. A soft plinking echoed in the grate nearby, and he realized the spider must have dropped down. He approached the grate cautiously. This was not the type he would normally enter. The drop was too far for a mouse to fall, but the metal creature was sturdier than a mouse of flesh and bone. He saw a glint of metal as the spider righted itself and disappeared in the darkness. *Drat,* he thought. There was no way to follow it.

Back at the lamp factory, he ducked inside his nest. It was a cozy place, situated inside the factory wall. He'd found enough scrap fabric from the lady workers to build a nice soft bed. The line that supplied heat to the main factory room ran right through this section of wall, so winter was easy on the little mouse. It was a perfect home, safe and warm. As he licked the sticky sweetness from his paws, he wished his stomach were bigger so he could eat some more. It would just have to wait. Crossing the factory floor, he made his way to the little flap on the door to Cali's apartment.

Pausing outside of it, he realized that he'd always avoided this opening. What mouse would want to get close to a cat? Especially an enhanced cat. Emmit let out a soft laugh, amused by his situation. Instead of mortal enemies, the two had come together in what he now considered friendship. *A strange friendship indeed,* he mused before letting himself in.

Cali's ears perked up at the squeak of hinges. "Who's there?" she called. Slinking low across the apartment, she searched for signs of heat. Her tensed muscles relaxed as she recognized the shape of a mouse. "Emmit," she said. "What have you found?"

"Greetings," the mouse said cheerfully. "I wanted to tell you that Morcroft has repaired his door and placed a new lock on it. I don't think we'll be able to get in that way again. It's rigged to explode."

"Did you look for another way in? We might very well need access to that workshop."

"I didn't," the mouse admitted. Why hadn't he thought to look for one? The news did her little good without an alternate route inside. "I'll check the area for a window or a path through the sewers." He doubted he'd find one, but he still scolded himself for not looking. Morcroft's office was secure, his privacy a serious concern. He wouldn't want anyone to be able to get inside without his knowledge.

"Is that all?" Cali asked.

"One more thing," Emmit told her. "There was an automaton, a spider. It was carrying something shiny."

"A clockwork spider?" she asked. "What on earth?" The finding wasn't suspicious. It was absurd. Who would want such a thing? Most people were terrified of spiders. Cali didn't mind them. They had a nice crunch to them.

"I couldn't follow it," Emmit said, disappointed. "It disappeared in the sewers where I couldn't enter."

Cali scratched a claw against her chin. Could Morcroft have created the spider? "You don't know what it was carrying?"

"It was round and shiny," the mouse replied. "Probably metal."

"A coin?" Cali offered.

"That's it!" Emmit said, excited. "I don't know why I didn't think of it. Yes, it must have been a coin."

"That still doesn't make any sense," she said. "What would a clockwork spider need with a coin? Did someone drop it, and the spider was returning it? Or was the spider sent to retrieve it?"

"I didn't see it pick up the coin," Emmit replied.

"It's all right," Cali said. She gave the mouse a reassuring pat on his back. "Keep your eyes peeled and let me know if you see any more of those spiders." They were probably nothing. Some tinker was likely experimenting, and that's all there was to it. "I appreciate your help, Emmit."

Leading the way to the kitchen, she hopped onto the table and unwrapped a small cloth bundle. Inside was a bit of cheese. Emmit's eyes gleamed as he saw it. Deep orange in color, its rich scent called out to him.

"For me?" the mouse asked.

"Yes indeed," Cali replied. "All yours."

It was far too large for Emmit to carry in one piece, and his stomach was too full of honey roll to eat much more. Making a little room, he nibbled at the edge of the cheese, savoring its freshness. Cheese was usually hard and possibly molded by the time it came to him. This was a treasure beyond all expectation.

"I can help you carry it back to your home if you like," Cali offered. She knew it was too large for the little mouse to carry alone.

"That'd be lovely," Emmit replied.

Grasping the cheese in her mouth, Cali followed the mouse through the factory and tucked the cheese inside his nest. She found it odd that she hadn't noticed the small, asymmetrical hole in this portion of wall. It was directly behind Florence's desk. Being so well-fed had obviously lessened her mousing skills. As she returned to her apartment, Cali wondered if she was still capable of being an effective mouser. She would surely never look at a mouse quite the same way again.

Chapter 8

"Cali wake up! There's another spider, and it's not far from here!" Emmit's little paws dug into the furry feline's side.

The calico awoke with a start, nearly jumping straight out of her skin. Blinking the sleep away, she repeated, "Spider? Spider!" Opening the window, she said, "Take me to it."

Emmit led the way, galloping along the street and dodging the feet of several passersby. Cali remained hot on his heels. Three blocks away, Emmit paused midstride.

"Did you find it?" she asked, scanning the area with her enhanced eye. She saw no trace of anything mechanical or otherwise.

"I-I…" he stammered. Spinning around, he looked down the alleyway. Defeated, he said, "I lost it."

Swallowing her disappointment, Cali said, "It's all right, Emmit. There's no telling where the thing was going. And I'm sure it's faster than a mouse with all those legs." Sniffing at the air, she decided to go for a prowl. She could spot one of the automatons from a farther distance than Emmit with his small eyes. "I'm going for a look around," she said. "You want to come along?"

"We're not too far from Morcroft's," Emmit said. "I'll check around over there first and meet up with you afterward."

"Good idea," Cali replied. "I'll head that direction." She pointed off to the left. "If you can't find me, just wait for me at the apartment."

Nodding, Emmit scampered off across the street. Cali kept her shoulders low as she headed down the alley. Wet newspapers littered the narrow path, but there was no sign of the spider. Her senses tingled, all setting themselves to high alert. These spiders were a sign of something bigger, and she'd bet anything that Morcroft was behind them. He had probably wanted Lionel to construct them for him. Whatever he was doing, she had to find out before it caused more danger for her friend.

Emerging into the sunlight, Cali spotted Nellie's carriage. *Perfect timing,* she thought.

"Hello again," the calico called to her.

"Cali!" Nellie said with a neigh. "Just the cat I wanted to see. I have news to report."

"What is it?" Cali asked, planting herself on the sidewalk next to the horse.

"I saw the oddest thing," the black-and-white horse began. "It looked like a spider, except it was all metal and had a small winding mechanism on its back."

"You're not the first to tell me about them," Cali said. "Where was it?"

"Less than a block from Morcroft's workshop," Nellie replied. "But its location wasn't as strange as its actions."

I knew it, Cali thought. *Morcroft is behind this.* "Tell me," the calico implored.

"It climbed up a gentleman's pant leg, snatched a small purse from his pocket, and fled." The horse recounted the tale with a shudder. Clearly the incident had unnerved her. "I whinnied and tried to get my master's attention, but he rubbed my nose and told me to calm down. He didn't see a thing."

"Humans are like that," Cali replied. "Did you happen to see where the spider went after it stole the purse?"

"I did," the horse replied proudly. "It tucked into a tiny flap in Morcroft's door."

Wrinkling her brow, Cali wondered if Emmit had missed something when visiting Morcroft's workshop. "I thought the new door was sealed tight and armed."

"New door?" Nellie wondered. "No this is the same door that's always been there."

An idea came to Cali. "Wait a minute," she said. "Where is Morcroft's workshop?"

Nellie gestured straight forward with her nose. "Three blocks ahead, make a right, then go two blocks and turn left. Third building on your right."

Cali's mouth gaped open. *He has a second workshop.* "Thank you, Nellie. You've been most helpful."

"Happy to help," the horse replied.

Flicking her tail, Cali darted across the street, wondering if she should retrieve Emmit before heading to Morcroft's alternate workshop. To her surprise, he found her first. His voice squeaked from the distance, her ears straining to make out the words.

"Cali!" Emmit called. "Come quick!"

Bounding forward on enhanced legs, Cali sped toward him. "What's wrong?" she cried.

Pointing with his tail, the little mouse directed her attention to a brass spider scurrying along the sidewalk. The clockwork creature moved with an odd gait. Three of its legs appeared to be slightly shorter than the others, throwing it off balance. If Morcroft built it, he did so in a hurry. Lionel would never have been satisfied with such shoddy workmanship.

Emmit started forward, but Cali reached out a paw to stop him. "Wait," she said, her voice no louder than a whisper.

Stumbling along its way, the spider twisted its head side to side. It paused for a moment, then started moving again.

What is it up to? Cali's muscles tensed, aching to pounce. *Patience,* she reminded herself. She had to see what the spider was planning.

A man and woman linked arm in arm appeared on the sidewalk. They strolled casually along, enjoying the fine air, completely unaware of the spider heading their way. Cali and Emmit sat perfectly still, waiting and watching.

Folding its legs, the spider shortened its height by half. Low to the ground, it crept along. Zooming in with her mechanical eye, Cali saw what appeared to be pads on the bottom of its feet. The creature was now moving with silent steps. As it hopped onto the woman's skirt, she realized the foot pads were also used for gripping.

"Look!" Emmit squeaked. The spider was making its way up the woman's back. With delicate arms, it reached out to unhook the necklace she wore, slipping it over its own head.

That was all Cali needed to see. Bounding forward, she timed her pounce to catch the spider as it descended the woman's dress. A powerful leap sent the calico flying through the air, a yowl of displeasure sounding from her throat. *Thwack!* She landed square on top of the spider, pinning it in place. The woman screeched in surprise, tumbling face first to the ground. Cali sat atop her back, wrestling with the clockwork spider. Metal legs thrashed as the spider tried to free itself. It was no use. Cali clamped her jaws tight, refusing to let go.

"Shoo, now!" the man shouted. "Out of here!" He swatted a hand at her as he reached down to help the woman back to her feet.

This was no time to hang around. Slipping the necklace loose with her claw, she dropped it on the woman's back. Dashing across the street, she waved her tail at Emmit. The mouse got the message and followed. Together they raced toward the factory, the spider kicking all the while. Outside her window, Cali shook the automaton and clamped down harder, hoping to still its constant thrashing. It didn't work.

Entering the window with Emmit close behind, Cali tried to speak through a mouthful of spider.

"Gamp bebbid oose," she said.

"I didn't quite catch that," Emmit replied.

Spitting out the spider, she quickly clamped a paw over it, pressing down with all her weight. "I can't let it loose," she said. "It's too tough for me to break it, and if I let it run free, there's no telling what trouble it will cause in here."

"Let me see," the mouse replied. "Maybe it has an off switch." Running his mousey fingers over the metal, he found a small switch on the spider's back.

Holding his breath, he flipped it to the opposite position. He sighed with relief as the spider ceased its struggling and fell dormant.

"I'm glad that was an off switch and not a 'go crazy' switch," Cali commented, meowing with laughter.

"Cali? Is that you?" a voice called from the front door.

Surprised by the sudden sound, Emmit nearly fell off the windowsill. Cali's ears perked up. She recognized the voice.

"It's Lionel," she told the mouse.

Trotting toward the door, she greeted her friend, rubbing her face against his legs. She hadn't expected him to return so soon. Yet here he was, hard at work on the new locking mechanism.

Running back to the window, she retrieved the spider and dropped it at Lionel's feet. With a *mrrrowww* she called his attention to it.

"What have you got there?" he wondered. The last gift she'd delivered had been a half-dead shrew. Adjusting his glasses, he examined the metallic device. "Hmmm," he commented, carrying the spider to his work table. Setting it amongst the clutter, he searched for the correct tool. Finding it, he said, "Let's see what we've got."

As Cali sat silent, Lionel opened the spider's back, revealing the inner workings. Gears and springs were nestled inside, the faint scent of burnt oil causing her nose to wrinkle. Lionel reached for a magnifying glass and pinned it to his glasses. Several minutes of careful inspection passed. Cali laid down at his feet, wondering what he was thinking.

Eventually he reached for a second tool, a slender rod of metal with a star-shaped end. Inserting it in the spider, he worked at it for a moment before removing a small gear. "I knew it," he said. He gazed at the gear for a moment before holding it out toward Cali. "This right here is a proprietary gear," he announced.

Cali wasn't sure what that meant. She stared at him blankly, awaiting an explanation.

Lionel was happy to oblige. "These symbols right here are the mark of none other than Jamison Morcroft. This is his patented gear mechanism. It uses wound springs for power in addition to a special oil." Frantically he began prying apart the metal creature's head. "Just as I thought," he said. A tiny light blinked inside. "That right there is how it sees. Not anywhere near as well as you, Cali, but good enough for its purpose."

Meowing, Cali tried to tell him to go on with his explanation. Asking him directly wasn't an option, and her curiosity was not yet satisfied. If only humans could understand the speech of animals.

Lionel set the spider aside and replaced his tools amid the clutter. Cali feared she would not get her explanation. She padded back to the windowsill and sat next to Emmit while Lionel went back to work on the door.

A gentle rapping from the rear entrance could only mean one thing. Cali sprang back to her feet, anxious to hear what Lionel would say to his sister.

"How was your trip?" Florence asked as she stepped inside. "Did you get the parts you needed?"

"Sure did," Lionel replied. "I'd like to see anyone break into this door now." Holding up his index finger, he stepped outside and pulled the door shut. "Flip that switched to the armed position," he called from the other side.

Florence obeyed and took two steps away from the odd looking device. "Ready," she called back.

Lionel tried the knob, which would not turn completely thanks to the lock. But it didn't end there. He shoved against it with all his weight, diving at it and kicking it. The door didn't budge, but a small ball bearing jostled loose, tumbling its way along a series of crooked ramps.

Cali and Florence watched, their heads following the motion of the ball as it dropped all the way to the wooden floor. It landed with a plunk, striking a small lever that neither of them had noticed previously. The lever clicked on, a bright blue light surrounding the edges of the door. Lionel could see the light from his side as well.

"It works!" he shouted. A thin blue current blinked to life, sparks dancing and flying in all directions. "Anyone who touches that will wish they hadn't," he said with pride. "You can switch it off with the lever behind the lamp."

Florence examined the wall, and sure enough, there was a small lever sticking out behind the lamp. With a flick of the switch, the lights vanished, rendering the door safe once again.

Lionel stepped back inside, his arms wide, a broad smile on his face.

"That's all well and good for the apartment," Florence pointed out, "but what about when you're out in the streets? He could still send his men to grab you again."

"I've solved that too with a personal beacon," Lionel said, smiling. "It works similar to Cali's recall device. Except instead of alerting me, it sounds a siren that can be heard a mile away. It also sends out an electric charge that will stun anyone who lays hands on me."

"Will it stun you as well?" she asked, concerned.

"Not at all," he said. "You know how you can rub your feet on the carpet and give someone a good shock?"

"Yes," she replied, remembering how he used to delight in playing that trick on her when they were children.

"You can touch yourself all day long, and it doesn't shock you. It only shocks when you touch the other person."

"If I remember correctly, it shocks both people," she stated. "And it's quite uncomfortable." Her worry for her brother was genuine. He was a brilliant man, but he could get in a hurry and not think things all the way through.

"I said it wouldn't *stun* me," he replied. "It *will* shock me, but only a little. I'd let you touch it, but I don't want to hurt you. Trust me, though. It works exactly as I've intended it to."

Her lips turned downward, but she decided to accept him at his word. All of his inventions were a secret, even to her. He would never fully explain how it worked, and she wouldn't ask. His business was his own, and she had little interest in gears and levers.

"Let me show you what Cali found," Lionel said, changing the subject. Lifting the spider off his table, he held it out to his sister.

Florence took the contraption in her gloved hand and wrinkled her brow. "What is it?" she asked.

"A spider," he replied.

Jumping backward, she dropped the metal arachnid to the ground.

"Not a real one," he said, laughing. Stooping low, he retrieved the gadget and placed it back on the table. "Morcroft crafted it. It's made to steal things."

"How do you know?" she asked.

Cali's ears perked up. Finally she was about to have her question answered.

"I know it's him because his name and patent number are engraved on one of the gears," Lionel explained. "It has a primitive brain, one I designed years ago. It has room for only the tiniest program, though."

"What did Morcroft program it to do?" she wondered, her eyes lingering on the metal spider.

"Find and retrieve is the simplest answer," Lionel replied. "I designed these to retrieve components for watchmakers. They're small and delicate enough for such work. Morcroft has altered the design. Now it looks for coins and jewels."

"How do you know?" she asked.

"Because it's my design," he replied. "I can see the changes he's made." Lifting the spider, he pointed to three tiny rivets. Still blinking, the small white light searched for its treasure. When he held it near a tool, one of the rivets reflected the light. Moving it near the lamp, it reflected two rivets. Holding it up to Florence's emerald earring, the third rivet lit up, and a triangular beam shot across the mechanical brain.

Gasping, Florence placed her hand on her heart. "That's amazing," she said. "I've never seen anything so strange."

"And criminal," Lionel added. "Not only did he steal my design, he's using these things to pilfer money and jewels from unsuspecting citizens."

"Morcroft is a wealthy man," Florence pointed out. "Why would he need to steal money?"

"Beats me," Lionel answered.

Cali glanced over at Emmit, a look of understanding passing between them. Morcroft didn't need the money at all. He was preparing for something else—something much bigger.

Chapter 9

Beams of silver moonlight glinted off Cali's brass fittings, giving her an otherworldly glow. Pacing outside the window, she strained her ears, listening for any sign of Emmit. When he finally showed himself, he was licking at his paws.

"You're late," she scolded.

"Dinner took longer than expected," he replied with a shrug. "It's not like we need to hurry over to

Morcroft's. Unless you've figured out a way to disarm his explosives."

"I have some news," Cali said. "I spoke to Nellie, and she saw one of the spiders—"

"Wait, Nellie who?" Emmit asked.

"She's the black-and-white horse who pulls the carriage with the tassels on the roof," Cali explained.

"Oh, I see," the mouse replied. "Please, go on."

"Nellie saw one of the spiders go into Morcroft's workshop, and it wasn't the workshop we knew about. He has a second one."

Emmit's eyebrows shot up. "Lead the way then."

Skulking along beneath the moonlight, Cali kept close to the walls. There were several people out this night, all of them dressed in their finest. A princess from a remote island on the Sapphire Sea had come to Ticswyk, and a grand moonlight ball was planned in her honor. Princess Kaleyani would spend the evening surrounded by the citizens of Ticswyk, and Cali had a feeling that Morcroft would be there as well. With any luck his workshop would be left unattended, giving her and Emmit plenty of time to have a look around.

Following Nellie's directions to the workshop, the calico did her best to stay out of sight. There could be no delays, even by people who wanted to admire her.

She saw many individuals looking at her with interest, but there was no time to stop. Her heart yearned for simpler times, when a cat could just be a cat. But tonight she had to be more. Lionel hadn't given her such amazing abilities to sit around idle.

Not only was her dearest friend in danger, all of Ticswyk could be Morcroft's target. It was up to Cali to figure it out before the sinister man could make his move. Luckily she was not alone. She had Emmit, who had proved his worth many times over. Resourceful and intelligent, Cali couldn't have asked for a better companion.

Travel proved slower than Cali liked. She grew impatient, and darted between the legs of couples as they strolled along the street. Emmit had to hold onto her tail to keep the pace and stay safe. More than one person stumbled, thanks to Cali's weaving in and out. But the calico never slowed nor looked back. Tripping people was sometimes unavoidable when a cat needed to get where she was going.

Since the carriages were operating late tonight, crossing the street took some time. Darting across wasn't an option. They had to wait until the way was clear. The clock at Exhibition Center chimed the hour, each clang echoing in her ears. Time was wasting, and she was still blocks away from the workshop.

Finally, the crowds dispersed, most of them having reached their destination. This corner of the city was virtually deserted, leaving Cali and Emmit free to prowl straight to Morcroft's door.

"I should have known this place," Emmit commented.

"Why's that?" Cali asked.

"Over there is the creamery," he said, pointing across the street. "I go by there at least once a week to look for scraps." He paused to sniff the air. "Of course, I'm usually behind the building. I can't recall being on this particular street before."

"It doesn't matter," Cali said. "We're here now." Making use of her mechanical eye, she scanned the workshop door for any sign of weakness. At its base was a tiny flap, large enough for a mechanical spider to make its way inside. Indicating the flap with her claw, she said, "There's our entry." Grinning, she added, "Small enough for a mouse." She was certainly glad she hadn't chosen someone larger for her ally.

Gathering his courage, Emmit stepped forward and pressed his weight against the flap. It held fast. "The spiders must have some sort of key," he said.

"I see the lock," Cali said. Her mechanical eye zoomed in on a small opening, big enough for a metal spider's leg. A cat's claw could fit as well. Unsheathing one claw, she inserted the tip into the small keyhole. Working at the lock the way Emmit had done before, she heard a soft click. "Now try," she told him.

Giving the flap a push, it swung open with ease. "What am I looking for in there?" he asked.

"First, a way for me to get in," Cali said. "Then we can search the place together." She didn't want him in there alone too long. It was likely to be dangerous, and without her there to protect him, the mouse might come to harm. "If you don't find anything within three minutes, come back here and let me know."

"Will do," Emmit said. After a few deep breaths, he stepped inside the flap. Machines whirred and puffed, the scent of burnt oil nearly gagging him. His whiskers twitched while his beady eyes scanned the perimeter. There was no sign of a dog, thankfully, nor was there the scent of dog food anywhere nearby. He moved slowly, keeping his steps as quiet as possible. It wasn't until his head began to throb that he realized he'd been holding his breath. As quietly as he could, he let out the breath and tried to keep himself calm.

Like the other workshop, this one appeared to have no windows. There was another door, but it was wooden, and positioned where it could lead only to another room or hallway, not the outside. How was Cali to get inside? A glance upward revealed a vent, but Emmit had no way to remove the metal covering.

Returning to the door, he squeaked, "There's no other way in. You'll have to try to force the door."

"Do you think that's wise?" she replied. "We know about the explosives on the other door only because you saw them installed. This one could be rigged as well."

She made a valid point. "The only other way I saw was a vent, but I can't get to it. You'd have to remove the cover from the inside."

"It's worth a try," she said. "Where do you think it lets out?"

"There has to be a duct attached somewhere on the top of the building," Emmit told her. "I think the vent is meant to let out some of the foul air from the shop."

Great, Cali thought, remembering the scent of the sewers the mouse had led her through on their first journey together. "I'll check the roof," she said. "Wait for me."

Skirting the workshop's perimeter, Cali kept herself close to the bricks. There could be security devices out here, and she didn't want to be spotted. It could take a few minutes to find some evidence against Morcroft, and the last thing she needed was to set off an alarm.

A convenient drainpipe attached to the corner of the building made a perfect ladder. Sinking her metal claws into the pipe, she bounded upward. In three strides, she was on the flat roof. The vent's outlet rose only a foot above the roof in the shape of an upside-down L. She knew she wouldn't have any trouble getting inside. It was just wide enough for a cat.

Hopping inside, she slowed her descent by clinging to the metal with her claws. The racket caught Emmit's attention, and he stepped cautiously inside the workshop to see if it was Cali. When her purple eye gleamed at him from behind the vent cover, he knew she had found her way inside. With a rattle and a clang, she kicked her enhanced rear legs at the cover, shaking it loose from the wall. It clattered to the floor, skidding along with a metallic scratching sound. The little mouse cringed as it slid past him.

Cali hopped down from the high vent and landed silently on the concrete floor. "Not a bad way to go," she said.

Emmit thought it could have been quieter, considering their need for stealth. But he kept that opinion to himself and began searching. A quiet click caught his attention, and he froze in place.

"Did you hear that?" he asked. A second sound, clunking and heavy, as if a machine were flopping over and over resonated through the room.

"What was that?" Cali asked, despite knowing Emmit didn't have the answer.

They didn't have to wait long to find out. Sliding through the wooden door on three wheels was a small man crafted of bronze. Cast in a permanent crouched position, he looked entirely uncomfortable. But this man had no sense of comfort or pain. He was not alive by any sense of the word. No more than an automaton, he was built as a sentry and nothing more.

Cali and Emmit scrambled to the corner of the room, knowing the sentry must be avoided at all costs. Its single eye at the center of its head projected a slender ray of red light as it scanned the workshop for any sign of movement. They watched as it charted a path from one end to the other, turning to repeat the scan again and again.

"We'll have to time our movements so that thing doesn't spot us," Cali said. She wasn't about to let this simple machine keep her from her goal.

When the sentry turned its back, Cali flicked her tail and dashed across the room. Reaching a desk covered in papers and plans, she sifted through the stack. Emmit kept his eyes focused, checking each page as she tossed it aside. There was nothing about spiders to be seen.

Pausing on one plan, Cali held it close to her nose. Studying it closely, a memory clicked in her mind.

"Did you find something?" Emmit asked, peering at the paper. It was a drawing of some device resembling a cookie cutter. "Do you know what that is?"

"I do," she replied.

Before she could explain, the sentry's wheels swiveled, signaling it was turning around. The pair dashed back toward a dark corner to avoid it.

Still clutching the drawing, Cali said, "This is a lock that Lionel designed."

"So what?" Emmit replied. Morcroft was always stealing ideas, so it was no surprise he would have Lionel's plans.

"Look," Cali said, pointing to the schematic.

"Uh-oh," Emmit said. Written clearly on the plans were the words MAIN VAULT. This was the locking mechanism for the bank, one that secured its most precious treasures. "Morcroft must be planning to break into the bank."

"I think you're right," she said. Moving her paw, she revealed more writing on the bottom corner of the schematics. Tiny spiderlings, half the size of the ones they'd encountered, were depicted infiltrating the lock. "Are you thinking what I'm thinking?"

"That he's training even smaller spiders to unlock the vault?" Emmit guessed.

"Exactly," Cali replied. With Lionel's schematics, Morcroft knew exactly how the lock functioned. It was an extremely complex design, but that wouldn't matter with a dozen spiderlings inside it. They wouldn't have to decipher the lock, they'd only have to damage it enough to force it to release. Then Morcroft could waltz into the vault and take whatever he wanted. This was a dreadful discovery.

"I think we should put that back where we found it," Emmit suggested. "If he knows someone is onto his scheme, he might not act on it. Then we won't have a chance to catch him."

"Smart thinking," the cat replied, impressed. When the sentry pivoted around again, she leapt for the desk and replaced the schematics. A small leather journal caught her eye, and she flipped through it, looking for anything suspicious. Drawings of herself appeared halfway through, and she held the book open for Emmit to see.

"He's trying to figure out how you work," he said. A shiver ran along his spine as he stared at the drawings. The inner workings of any animal were not pleasant to look at. Through these drawings, Morcroft was experimenting with attaching metal implants to various parts of a cat's body. Some of them were quite graphic. Emmit turned away, unable to look any longer.

Cali slammed the book shut. Her first thought was to take it with her and destroy it. But Emmit made a good point. There should be no evidence that they were ever here.

A strange silence alerted Cali. The sentry's wheels no longer scratched against the concrete floor. Too late she realized they'd been paying attention to the book when the automaton swiveled around. Its red eye blinked as it spotted the intruders. A click followed by a low buzzing told Cali the system was arming itself.

Grabbing Emmit's paw, she leapt from the table, narrowly avoiding a small projectile. It struck the ground just short of the main door and exploded in a shower of sparks.

"We have to get out of here, now!" Cali cried. Before he could reply, she grabbed Emmit in her teeth and scrambled up the wall, her claws digging into the wood.

When they landed inside the vent, Emmit asked, "Shouldn't we replace the cover?"

As much as she hated to agree, Cali had no choice. If she left it open, Morcroft would know someone had broken in. "I'll get it," she said.

Another projectile exploded somewhere below, but Cali ignored it. Returning to the ground, she didn't bother to look for the sentry. Instead she raced across the floor and retrieved the vent cover. Grabbing it in her teeth, she turned and found herself face to face with the automaton. Leaping on its head, she avoided the next projectile. From there she sprang to the wall, digging her claws in as deep as she could. Climbing to the vent, she disappeared inside, snapping the cover in place behind her.

"That was close," she said.

Emmit sat against the vent wall, thinking. "I don't suppose we could clean up after those projectiles. That's sort of evidence too."

"I'm not going back down there," she replied. "Hopefully Morcroft will think the stupid thing fired on his spiders."

"You're probably right," Emmit replied. Since there was no other evidence of intruders, and automatons weren't all that smart, Morcroft would probably assume it had malfunctioned.

"Hold on tight," Cali said. Emmit grabbed onto her tail, and she lifted them through the vent toward the roof. "Don't let go yet," she warned him. Keeping her body low, she jumped down, landing on the sidewalk.

The drop tested the integrity of Emmit's stomach, but he endured it like a true professional. Cali's implants cushioned the landing, allowing her to dart away immediately. Racing back toward the factory, they both breathed a sigh of relief. Now that they knew what Morcroft was planning, they could focus their attention strictly on the bank. The moment things seemed amiss, they would spring into action. For now they were both grateful to have escaped with their lives. Sleuthing was dangerous work.

Chapter 10

After a night of much-needed rest, Cali rose feeling refreshed. Nightmares of the sentry had disturbed her dreams only once. She had fought it off, breaking it down into a million little spiderlings. One by one she and Emmit had eaten them all. Cali awoke feeling famished. The mouse was nowhere to be seen, having preferred to stay in his own home at the factory. He would probably be sleeping in.

Padding into the kitchen, Cali mewed softly at Lionel, who was already awake and reading his newspaper.

"Good morning," he called to her. "Your breakfast awaits." Remaining in his seat, he indicated with his head toward the kitchen.

A bowl of minced chicken with bits of cheese awaited, her eyes glistening at the sight of her prize. It was a rich breakfast, but one that was well-deserved. Her heroics from the night before had told her exactly what she needed to do. Of course, she'd need Emmit's help to do it. Taking two chunks of cheese and setting them aside, she dove in and devoured the rest. After hiding the mouse's portion, she returned to Lionel and twirled her tail around his ankles. He patted his leg, inviting her onto his lap. She curled up with him and enjoyed a few moments of peace and relaxation. Such moments seemed rare and precious lately.

Three taps sounded from the rear door, and Florence stuck her head inside. "Are you home?" she asked before stepping in.

"Of course," Lionel replied. "Come in, Flo." This time he did not greet her at the door, for fear of disturbing the calico still resting on his lap.

Florence approached and stroked Cali's fur before taking a seat of her own. Rummaging in a brown paper sack, she produced two pastries and handed one to her brother. "Tea cakes with strawberries and buttercream frosting," she announced. The woman had a voracious sweet tooth, and so did Lionel.

"How was the ball last night?" Lionel asked through a mouthful of cake.

"Delightful!" Florence replied. "The girls and I enjoyed every minute." Though unmarried, Florence wouldn't let a spectacular event like the princess's moonlight ball go by without attending. Though she hadn't arrived on the arm of a gentlemen, she had gathered her factory workers and arrived in style.

"Did anyone ask you to dance?" Lionel asked.

Blushing and turning her head to one side, she replied, "Well, as a matter of fact, yes. You remember Mr. Lisen? He and I shared a few dances."

"That fellow with the accent?" Lionel asked, trying to remember the man's face.

"He's the one," she said. "Striking blond hair too." Clearing her throat, she stopped herself before going into further detail. After all, a woman's heart is full of secrets, and she didn't care to share too much of it with her brother, even if he was among her dearest friends. "You should have come as well," she said, changing the subject.

"Not my sort of thing," Lionel replied. "Did you see the princess?" Turning his newspaper toward her, he pointed to a picture of the royal young woman.

"I did," Florence answered. "Princess Kaleyani is a beautiful woman with a generous heart. She presented the city of Ticswyk with her most prized possession, a golden owl. It was placed on display for all those in attendance to see. I've never seen such attention to detail. It even had diamonds for eyes. I'll bet it's worth more than half the city put together."

Her ears twitching, Cali could not ignore this news. Could this be what Morcroft was after? Was the statue being stored in the bank's vault? Scanning the newspaper, she tried to keep her actions concealed. Too much movement on her part and Lionel might get up and toss the paper away. She had to find the information. When she reached the end of the article without finding an answer, she sank back into his lap, defeated.

Finishing his dessert, Lionel came to the rescue. "What on earth would anyone need with such a gift?" he wondered. "They'll probably just tuck it away somewhere that no one will ever see it."

"Not true," Florence replied. "They announced it would be given a place of honor at every exhibition. In between shows it will be displayed at the museum."

Confused, Cali looked up and tilted her head to the side. Morcroft wasn't planning to rob the museum again. He was definitely planning to rob the bank's vault.

"The museum isn't secure enough for something of that value," Lionel commented. "They're still updating their security, and their construction has been slowed by the Guild's involvement. And between you and me, that floor isn't secure enough."

"Yes, but Mr. Lisen told me that until the museum was secured and a special exhibit designed for the owl, it will remain safely locked in the bank's vault." After chewing a small bite of cake, she added, "He's the bank's president, you know."

"Yes, I know," Lionel replied.

Cali couldn't believe her ears. That was it. Morcroft had some foreknowledge of the princess's gift and where it would be housed. Soon the museum would prove impenetrable. He had to steal it from the bank if he was going to steal it at all.

"Good thing the bank is secured by your own design," Florence commented.

"Yes, indeed," Lionel replied. "That gaudy bit of royal brass will be quite safe."

Cali knew better. The owl was in great danger. Morcroft would probably melt it down to rid himself of the evidence. Then he'd deposit it in his own account, piece by piece. As Lionel always said, "a wealthy man always desires more wealth." In this instance, at least, he was completely right.

Hopping down from Lionel's lap, Cali crossed through the apartment and headed out the rear flap. Inside the factory the ladies were hard at work. Only one took notice of Cali as she passed, calling out to the cat. Cali couldn't resist.

"How are you today, Miss Kitty?" the woman asked, leaning down to scratch the top of Cali's head.

Purring, Cali pushed her head into the woman's hand. From her pocket, the woman produced a handkerchief. Wrapped inside were a few crackers, which the woman broke into pieces and offered her. Cali accepted them gratefully. She held the last piece in her teeth before trotting away to see Emmit.

Florence was still visiting with Lionel, so there was no obstacle barring Cali from reaching her friend. Otherwise, the factory overseer would wonder what Cali was doing and might discover the little mouse's hiding place. Squeezing herself behind the desk, Cali dropped the cracker outside Emmit's door.

"Emmit," she called. "I brought you some breakfast."

The mouse's head appeared in the doorway. "Thanks, Cali!" he said, picking up the cracker and nibbling one edge.

"There's some cheese back at the apartment as well," she said. "I forgot it on my way out." News of the golden owl had shaken her, leaving her mind whirling. How was she going to prevent the heist?

Savoring the final bite of his cracker, Emmit took his time chewing. After it was gone, he licked his paws and wiped them on his fur. "Should I check the workshop this morning?" he asked.

Cali shook her head. "I think it would be better to keep an eye on the bank. There's definitely going to be activity there sooner or later." She wasn't sure if the spiderlings would exit the workshop and walk to the bank on their own, but if they did, they wouldn't be easily spotted. Morcroft would never take the chance of them being stopped before they reached their destination. In addition, they didn't know what route the spiders would take, and she didn't want to miss them along the way. Staying put at the bank seemed the wisest course of action.

"Why the bank?" Emmit wondered. He had yet to come across the day's headlines.

"I heard Lionel and Florence discussing it," Cali explained. "There's a golden owl in the bank's vault, and I'll bet anything that's what Morcroft is planning to steal."

After a moment's thought the little mouse nodded. It seemed like a logical target for Morcroft's scheming. "I'll head over there now and let you know if I see anything strange," he said.

"Actually," Cali said, "I have a better idea. Follow me."

Leading the way, the calico brought her mouse friend back to the apartment and through a door he hadn't noticed before. Inside was Lionel's workshop, a vast portion of the factory that was otherwise not in use. Cogs and gears larger than Emmit could imagine sat unmoving on the floor. Springs and scrap metal were heaped into neat piles, awaiting the tinker's next project.

On every wall, Emmit made note of various drawings, the schematics for Lionel's future inventions. Some of them looked more intricate than others. One in particular caught the mouse's eye. It appeared to be an engine for a balloon. The thought made him shudder. Balloons already traveled far too fast. He didn't want anywhere near the one Lionel was planning.

The calico led him over to a table, one of over a dozen in the room. She hopped up, climbing over books and papers. Opening the topmost drawer, she pulled out a tiny receiver. Smaller than a pocket watch and rectangular in shape, she proudly presented it to the mouse.

"This is how you can let me know if you see anything at the bank," she explained. "It's much faster than running back and forth."

Emmit ran a paw over the smooth metal. "What is it?" he asked. It certainly didn't look like anything special to him.

"It activates my homing beacon," she declared. "All you have to do is push this button at the center, and I'll know you need me."

"Are you sure it works?" he asked.

"Try it now," she urged him.

Since his paws alone weren't strong enough to press the button, he hopped on top of it, pressing down with his body weight. A tiny red light glowed to life at the tip of Cali's tail. Nodding his approval, Emmit said, "Nice."

"It might be a little heavy for you," Cali said. "I can strap it to you if you like."

"No, that will make walking awkward." Grabbing the button with his teeth, he tested the weight. "I think I can get it to the bank," he said.

"All right then," Cali replied. "Be careful, and don't hesitate to use that if you need me."

Emmit scurried off with the button in tow. Cali turned her attention back to the shop. There was one more item she needed, but she had no idea if it actually existed.

Studying every schematic posted on Lionel's walls, Cali came up empty. None of those inventions were what she needed. It wasn't surprising, though. Lionel hadn't needed any type of weapon until after his kidnapping. His mind didn't really think along those lines. Arming his front door had required a trip to a friend, one who knew about such things. Cali wished now that she had been along for the trip. Looking at the other inventor's plans might have taught her how to craft what she needed.

I'll just have to invent something myself, she decided.

Sifting through piles of different components, Cali's mind could not form any ideas. Sitting back on her haunches, she tried to think. What would she encounter at the bank? Spiderlings was the obvious answer. She had already seen them, drawn in Morcroft's own hand. They were tasked with opening the vault. Cali intended to be inside it, protecting the owl from mechanical thieves.

In her mind, Cali pictured the spiderlings attempting to carry the owl away. Then she realized something. The owl she had seen in the picture was too large and likely too heavy for such small creatures to carry away. Would Morcroft risk entering the vault in person? Cali doubted it. However, the spiderlings would have to be super strong to lift such weight, or they might instead be crushed by their prize. From the design schematics, Cali knew they were no sturdier than their larger counterparts.

That's when it struck her. The larger ones would be there as well, and it would still take a number of them to carry out the robbery. She wondered if Morcroft might be planning an even larger version that could easily lift the owl and carry it away. She needed to be prepared for whichever scenario she encountered.

Her mind whirled with possibilities, trying to decide what sort of weapon would be best. She couldn't carry a variety. That would leave her too loud and bulky to maneuver through the bank. If she was going to get into the vault, she'd have to rely on stealth. One weapon alone, and preferably something small, was all she could manage.

After a few moments in deep thought, Cali remembered the explosion that had let her out of Morcroft's workshop the night of Lionel's rescue. *That's it!* What she needed was a small, portable bomb. But she had to craft it with care. Blowing herself up was a real danger.

Darting around the workshop, she piled bits and pieces to experiment with. She made note of the location of some gunpowder but didn't dare to touch it yet. That was the most dangerous component, and she didn't want to risk an accidental explosion.

Choosing a small glass phial, Cali tapped it with her claws. It was sturdy, and unlikely to burst if carried near her implants. That was exactly what she needed. Next, she tested a few matches, making sure they were dry and in good working condition. Selecting two, she placed them next to the phial.

The third part of her invention took some searching to uncover. It had to be small enough to fit in the mouth of the phial, and rough enough to strike a match against. After digging through every inch of the workshop, she nearly turned a backflip when she found what she needed. A sheet of parchment coated in tiny bits of crushed glass would do the job perfectly. Normally used to smooth metal or wood surfaces, glass paper was the perfect abrasive surface. Tearing loose a tiny strip, she returned to her invention.

Making use of her claws, Cali fashioned her makeshift grenade. The cork stopper housed the matches, which were angled to strike against the edge of the phial's mouth. With a small drop of glue, she attached the glass paper to the phial's mouth, making sure the match heads would indeed come in contact with it. Testing her theory, she was delighted to see the matches spring to life. Blowing them out, she replaced them with two more.

Now came the most dangerous part. Carefully, Cali placed a small amount of gun powder inside the phial and packed strips of newspaper over the top of it. Making sure to twist the cap so the matches were on the opposite side of the glass paper, she stoppered the phial. Tucking it between sections of her tail implant, she made sure the grenade was held securely in place. It wouldn't do to have it rolling around loose. Now all she had to do was twist the stopper and pull it straight, thus striking the matches and lighting them. If all went as planned, the newspaper would catch fire and wick the flames, giving her enough time to throw her bomb before the flames hit the gunpowder. With a smirk, she thought, *That should stop those spiders in their tracks.*

Taking great pride in her invention, Cali strutted back toward the apartment. Before she could reach the door, the red light on her tail lit up. Emmit was in trouble.

Chapter 11

Tearing through the workshop, Cali paid no heed to the objects she knocked over. Sliding through the flap, she reentered the apartment only to hurl herself through the open window without stopping for a single breath. Emmit needed her, and that was all that mattered.

Cali's flight didn't stop from the moment her paws struck the sidewalk. It would take ten minutes by her estimate to reach the bank if she continued at this pace. That was no problem for a special cat like her. With her enhancements, she used far less energy than an ordinary cat, even while covering more ground. Her speed was unmatched by the casual feline, and her desire to save her friend further hastened her steps.

Dodging between carriages, she made a mad dash across the street. A horse reared back, halting the carriage and earning her a few gasps from the ladies inside. Back on the sidewalks her pace didn't slow. Sprinting for the alley, she weaved herself amid the crowds, navigating through their legs with expert skill. A man shouted and shook his fist as she flew past, nearly knocking him off-balance. She didn't bother to look back. No human could possibly hope to catch her. The red light on her tail gazed down at her, imploring her to run faster. What felt like hours passed, but in reality it was only minutes. She stopped short as she reached the bank, activating her mechanical eye.

Somewhere amid the humans coming and going was a mouse, and she had to find him. Was he still alive? Had he been injured? The worst scenario would be that he was carried off somewhere that she would never find him. Not knowing his fate would be the worst feeling of all. To her great relief, the figure of a warm mouse outlined against the cool grass entered her field of vision. Springing forward, she brought herself to his side.

"Are you hurt?" she asked, out of breath. He appeared uninjured to her eyes, but some wounds were undetectable by sight.

Emmit shook his head. "I'm sorry if I frightened you," he said, noticing her bristled fur. The calico was clearly shaken. He truly regretted worrying her.

"It's all right," she said, smoothing her fur and settling herself on her haunches. Seeing the mouse alive and well was more than she could have hoped for. "You summoned me," she said, awaiting an explanation.

"Yes," Emmit said. "Look over there." He pointed at man standing beside the bank and facing away from the street. He was short and plump with a brown derby hat pulled low to shield his eyes.

"Do you know him?" Cali asked. Despite the fact that she rarely forgot a face, she did not recognize this man.

"Never seen him before in my life," the mouse replied. "It's what he's carrying that made me summon you." He hoped Cali would find worth in his discovery. This man was definitely up to something. He'd been casing the outside of the bank ever since Emmit showed up.

The pair skirted around the edge of the grass, keeping clear of the road. A small natural park area near the bank gave ample cover. There were a few trees to hide behind, and a cat hanging around here wouldn't draw too much attention. Staying low to the ground, they kept themselves perfectly still. Not a single word passed between them, both understanding the need for absolute silence.

Concentrating only on the strange man, they tuned out every distraction on the street. His eyes darted all around nervously as he flicked a cigarette to the ground and stomped it with his boot. Then, he approached the bank's window, a small chest in his hands. Cali recognized it immediately from the previous night. Though it had stood open and empty in Morcroft's workshop, it obviously contained something now.

Neither spoke, instead a silent nod confirmed they had both seen the chest before. Staying intent on the scene in front of them, they could only guess what lurked inside. The heavyset man looked over his shoulder and to each side before opening the chest.

Cali zoomed in with her mechanical eye. Tiny, gold-colored dots crawled out of the box, clinging to the bank's outer wall. Further magnification revealed eight legs on each dot. Twelve clockwork arachnids walked in a row, making their way up the wall toward the open window. As they disappeared inside, the man shut the box and casually walked away.

"What did you see?" Emmit asked. His eyes were nowhere near as powerful as Cali's.

"Spiderlings!" she replied. "The smallest we've seen yet. He's let them loose in the bank. That means the heist is going down tonight!"

"What do we do?" Emmit squeaked. His first instinct was to run to the police, but they would never understand mouse-speak. He'd have to write it down first and deliver the message, never mind the strange looks they would give him. He could present them with the note and then run away, hoping that they'd believe him.

"We have to stop those spiderlings," Cali said.

"Ourselves?" Emmit asked. "Shouldn't we alert the police?" He had already worded the note in his mind.

"There's no time for that," she said. "And they'll never believe a cat and a mouse. They'll think it's some sort of prank."

Emmit knew she was probably right, but the two of them charging inside would be dangerous. They didn't know what Morcroft was planning. He might send in an army of dogs, all with enhancements like Cali's. They might end up as dinner rather than heroes. What they needed most was more time to plan. "I still think it's dangerous," he cautioned. "And how do you plan to get in without being seen? Those humans aren't going to want either of us in there."

"I know that, and I'll think of a way to slip in unnoticed," she replied. Her mind whirled with different scenarios, all of them ending in disaster. If she made it in, how would she avoid the security systems? Were they programmed to attack cats? Who or what would Morcroft send to fetch the owl? Would she be able to fight against it?

Double checking the security of her homemade weapon, she wished she'd had time to make ten of them. This mission was dangerous, no doubt about it. But she was in too deep to turn back now. She had to get inside the bank and protect the owl. Sending power to her haunches, her rear end wiggled as she prepared to pounce inside the window.

"Wait!" Emmit cried. "Look!"

He'd spotted the spiderlings straight ahead. They were making their way onto the bank manager's desk. A lady entered with a tray bearing a steaming pot of tea along with a ceramic cup. The banker acknowledged her with a nod, but didn't look up from his work. He had no idea the spiderlings were approaching.

"Do you think they'll hurt him?" Emmit whispered.

Cali didn't know how to answer. Narrowing her eyes, she kept watch over the clockwork devils. They crept along the desk, up the side of the banker's cup and did not exit again. She covered her mouth with her paw. "Morcroft wants the man to swallow them?" What on earth was he planning?

"They'll eat him from inside out!" Emmit squealed. "We have to do something."

"I agree," Cali said. "Do you think you can get inside and knock the cup over?"

"I think so," he answered. As long as the banker didn't look up, he would never see the mouse creeping along his desk. Otherwise, Emmit could be in big trouble.

"I'll be there in two hops if you get into trouble," Cali reassured him. It was a promise she intended to keep. Seen or not seen, she would get through the window and save her friend. Then if she was tossed from the bank by human hands it wouldn't matter. Emmit's safety was her first priority.

"I'm going in," the mouse said. He disappeared in a flurry of blue-gray fur, scampering along the window ledge and dropping down to the floor.

Cali saw his small form hurrying along near the banker's legs, pausing momentarily to make sure the man was distracted. He showed no signs of moving, so Emmit continued on his mission. His heart nearly stopped when the banker turned and reached for the tea pot. Tipping it over the cup, he filled it to the brim, the spiderlings nearly floating over the edge. A look of horror flashed across the mouse's face as he looked back at Cali. Flicking her paw, she signaled for him to hurry.

Dashing up the side of the desk, Emmit seated himself on top of a ledger. The banker's hand reached for the mug, grasping its handle in his hand. Panicking, Emmit didn't know what to do. Staying invisible was now impossible. He couldn't get to the cup without the man seeing him. Leaping for the cup, he slammed into its side. Grasping with his paws, he managed to hang on.

The bank manager, Mr. Lisen, took one look at the mouse and shouted, flinging the cup away. Mouse, spiderlings, and all sailed across the room, clattering to the floor. Cali wasn't sure where to look first. The spiderlings skittered away, hiding themselves between the slats of the wooden floor. Emmit raced away in the opposite direction with Lisen hot on his heels.

"Run, Emmit!" Cali shouted with a distressed yowl. Fearing she'd sent the mouse to his death, she pulled herself through the window.

Charging in the direction she last saw Emmit, she found herself on the edge of chaos. In the bank's central chamber, she saw a flash of fur as the little mouse tried desperately to evade his pursuers. One woman shrieked and jumped on top of her desk, giving Emmit the opening he needed. He darted beneath the desk, his heart pounding.

The relief lasted only momentarily. One man grabbed a broom and began poking it underneath the desk. Emmit was forced from his hiding space, frantically zigzagging through the room. There were too many wide open spaces. With nowhere to hide, he knew he'd soon be caught. It was only seconds before he found himself trapped. Paralyzed with fear, he crouched low near the wall.

A flash of purple revealed Cali at the far corner of the room. *I hope she has a plan*, he said to himself. He was completely out of ideas. Five men closed in around him, one still armed with the menacing broom.

The sudden crash of breaking glass diverted the men's attention. Unfortunately, Emmit was still frozen in place. His beady eyes landed on a painting of an arrogant, large-nosed man that had been dislodged from the wall in spectacular fashion. He heard the men asking how it had happened, but they weren't distracted for long. Turning their attention back to the mouse, they resumed their attack.

"Cali, do something!" he cried. His words sounded like a high-pitched squeal to the men in front of him.

"Squealing won't save your dirty little hide," the man with the broom said. Poking the bristles roughly at the mouse, he forced Emmit onto his hind legs.

Another picture fell from the wall, a blur of calico disappearing like a ghost. A framed map of Ticswyk shattered on the ground, shredding the fine details of the city. It still wasn't enough. Two of the men didn't even look away from the mouse.

Cali frantically searched for anything that would create a bigger diversion. Spotting an eight-foot-tall potted palm tree, she knew she'd found the answer.

Leaping for the top, she grabbed onto its wide leaves, tugging with all her might. As it began to topple, she bounced once against the trunk, lunging toward the ceiling. A dangling mass of crystal and silver nearly blinded her, but she grabbed a hold, ignoring the flashing light. Dangling from the chandelier, she watched as the tree crashed into the back of the man with the broom.

Scampering away, Emmit finally found safety. Off to his left was a marble statue of what appeared to be a tiger in attack posture. Situating himself between the statue and the wall, he prayed no one had seen him. When no one followed, he dared to breathe again.

While all the humans were focused on cleaning up the mess of palm tree, Cali flung herself from the chandelier. Somersaulting through the air, she landed next to the statue where the mouse had taken refuge. Joining him, she flattened herself against the floor.

Before she could ask if he was unharmed, a single *plunk* sounded at the center of the room. It was soon followed by a second and third. With no more warning, a great downpour of crystal and silver beads clattered to the floor, sending the humans slip-sliding all over.

"Now that's a distraction," Emmit commented. "Next time I'll think bigger."

Cali pressed a paw over her mouth to stifle her laughter. It wasn't exactly what she had in mind, but it would do. Everyone was far too busy with the cleanup to bother looking for the mouse now. Cali doubted anyone had seen her, as she'd taken great care with each leap. Bouncing from wall to wall, she'd focused her attention upward, above the humans' natural eye level.

"Did you see where the spiderlings went?" she asked.

"No," he replied. "I lost all sight of them after I started to run." Had he stopped for even a moment, he knew the humans would have had him. They would have smacked him with that broom and tossed his limp body out for wild animal predators to enjoy. It was a good thing Cali had come in behind him and caught their attention. "Thanks for saving me," he said.

"Any time," she replied.

"What do we do now?" Emmit asked.

"You have to get out of here," she said. "Go now while everyone is still cleaning up. By the time they're finished, it will be closing time. Get out the window before they lock it up tight."

"What are you going to do?" he wondered. Was she really going to stay in here alone and face whatever Morcroft sent inside?

"I've got to find a way in the vault," she said. "That's where the owl is, so that's where I have to be if I'm going to protect it." She'd already formed half a plan in her mind. The rest she'd have to figure out as she went along. For starters, she needed a way inside the vault. For now, the door stood open, but she couldn't exactly waltz inside. Two guards stood at their posts, unfazed by the strange events unfolding inside the bank. One stood next to the vault door, the other inside the vault itself. Distracting these professionals was going to take more than a chandelier.

"But those spiders are dangerous," Emmit protested. "Not to mention whatever Morcroft is sending to fetch the owl. It could be that sentry from his workshop. I think I should stay with you." Eventually the spiderlings would work their way back out of the floor, and they might want revenge.

"No," she replied. "I need you outside. There's something very important I need you to do."

Chapter 12

"What do you need, Cali?" Emmit asked, steeling himself for what she might say. So far he'd been courageous, but now that they were inside the bank, things seemed awfully bleak. At any moment, Morcroft might show up. Or worse, his creations might show up. Who knew what he was planning? He might take down the walls to get in. Those little spiderlings might only be a diversion.

"I need you to find the transmitter to light up my homing beacon," she told him.

Surprised, Emmit replied, "I know exactly where I left it." It was still on the grass beneath the windowsill where it was unlikely to be found by humans.

"Good," she responded. "You have to keep watch for me. Whenever Morcroft's thieves show up, press the button. Then I can be prepared."

"But it lets you know only that something is about to happen. It can't tell you what I've seen." How could she prepare if she didn't know what was happening? Emmit didn't like this plan at all. It was incomplete, not to mention dangerous.

"It won't make much difference what he sends in here," she replied. "I've already thought it through. I expect he'll send those spiders in. Why else train them to steal?"

"You're probably right," the mouse conceded. "But what if they're giant spiders instead of small ones?"

"Giant clockwork spiders would be unsteady and slow," she said. Her confidence renewed, she stuck out her chest. "You saw the way the smaller ones moved. Building them larger would only make their skittering, sloppy movements worse."

She made a good point. The calico was nimble and quick. Those spiders were no match for her. Besides, they were crafted to steal and flee, not stand and fight. At least, the ones they had seen didn't seem capable of defense. It was enough to put Emmit's mind somewhat at ease. With any luck, the bank thieves would not be more sophisticated than their smaller counterparts.

"While you're out there," Cali went on, "make note of any strange people or automatons. Don't approach them or put yourself in danger, but if they're doing something they shouldn't, try to stop them or at least slow them down."

Emmit's beady eyes stared blankly at the cat. What she asked would be impossible. He couldn't try to stop someone from suspicious activity without putting himself in danger. Rather than argue the point, he nodded instead.

"Keep yourself hidden," she warned. "I don't want anyone or anything attacking you while I'm inside the vault."

"How do you plan to get in there?" he asked.

"I'll have to find a way to distract the guards," she said.

"I could have a go at them," he offered. He'd survived his last run through the bank. What harm could a second one do?

Cali shook her head. "I don't want you putting yourself in that situation again." There was no longer a chandelier for her to grab onto, and she needed to conserve her energy if she hoped to stop the robbery that was about to take place. "I'll find my own way in," she said. Flashing a set of white teeth, she added, "Trust me."

Emmit smiled. He did trust her. She was clever and strong, and she could most definitely look out for herself. There was really no reason to worry about her, though he still felt some apprehension. Posted outside, he wouldn't be able to witness the events taking place in the bank. What if she needed him? *I'll just have to do the best I can from outside,* he decided. *If I know she's in real trouble, I'll come in anyway.* His mind was made up. "I guess I'll head out the window then," he said. "Unless you need anything else before I go?"

"I'll be fine," she said, patting him on top of his head. "Remember, don't let anyone see you."

Nodding, he looked all around before dashing across the room and back into the manager's office. Bouncing first to the desk and then onto the windowsill, he looked back at Cali crouching behind the statue. Her calico fur was neat and tidy, despite the ordeal she'd been through to save him. *A true hero,* he thought. He was proud to call her his friend. Hopping down from the window, he stood watch next to the transmitter.

Keeping a low profile, Cali did not emerge from behind the statue. The guards stood their ground while the cleanup continued, preventing her from entering the vault. A small bead of crystal rolled near her, and she decided to give throwing it a try. Lifting it in her enhanced paw, she tossed it toward the nearest guard. It struck the side of his neck, but the man didn't even flinch. Cali could hardly believe it. Most people would have at least lifted a hand to see what had hit them. Not this guard. She'd have to try something else.

The only other thing within reach was the homemade explosive tucked into her implants. Throwing that was out of the question. She didn't want to injure the guards, just move them long enough to get herself inside the vault.

Tapping a claw against her chin, she waited for an opportunity to present itself. Nearly an hour went by, and still nothing. The guards did not take breaks, nor did they shift their attention away from the vault.

Apparently it was nicely protected. She wondered if she was being foolish by staying. Surely Morcroft couldn't get past them.

As the afternoon went on, Cali grew drowsy. Taking a nap was a tempting idea. No one had noticed her behind the statue, so it was unlikely she'd be discovered, awake or asleep. Yawning, she let out a long sigh. *I have to stay awake,* she told herself. What if she fell into a deep sleep and missed the entire heist? Morcroft would get away with the theft, and she'd have to admit to Emmit that she'd been snoozing on the job.

Curling her arms beneath her, Cali settled in for a long wait. Instead of sleeping, she observed the people around her. Customers came and went, exchanging pleasantries with the tellers. Some left with small bundles of cash, others left empty-handed. Cali hoped one would enter the vault. If so, she might be able to tag along unnoticed. But no such luck. Not one person expressed an interest in going inside it.

A quiet crinkling from beneath the floor gave her a start, and she stood back up on all fours. She saw nothing, but the noise continued. Dropping down again, she pressed an ear to the wood. The sound grew louder and then turned away in the direction of the vault. It had to be the spiderlings. They were on the move again. She wondered why they would do so now, after hours of remaining dormant. Then she realized that, like her, they were waiting for the right moment. Something was about to happen.

The bank manager emerged from his office with a flat leather bag under his arm. Setting the bag aside, he motioned to a lady teller. She began removing money from her cashbox, and two other tellers followed suit. Cali watched with interest, wondering what would happen next. When the tellers were ready, they brought the cash to Lisen, who tucked the money in the bag and proceeded toward the vault.

Could this be the moment? Cali positioned herself for a pounce. The banker walked past the first guard, who immediately took up a position in the center of the open vault door. Cali weighed her options. The door was circular and quite large. There was plenty of room for her to fit around the guard. The trouble was, there was no cover. He would see her before she made it in. She could grab onto the banker's leg, but he'd definitely feel it and shake her off before going in the vault.

When the manager disappeared inside the vault, she realized she'd missed her chance. Sitting back on her haunches, she wondered what would happen when he emerged. Several minutes passed, and Cali grew impatient. She stuck one paw from behind the statue, but the guard flinched, and she feared she'd been seen. Making herself small, she hunkered back down in her hiding place.

When Lisen emerged, he was followed by the second guard. *Success!* Cali thought. Now there was only one guard to deal with. When the outer guard joined the other two, her heart lifted. The three stopped at a mechanism on the wall next to the vault door.

Panicking, Cali realized what was happening. The bank was closing. That's the only reason the guards would leave their posts. They were about to secure the massive door, and she'd lose any chance of getting inside before the spiderlings.

A loud hiss echoed through the bank, a signal that the door's latch had been released. It was now or never. Cali braced herself, shifting all her power to her hind quarters. She had to avoid the heavy door as it swung closed on its own, moving faster as it neared its destination. The door's jagged edge would have to be avoided as well, requiring some maneuvering on her part.

Steadying her breathing, she forced herself to wait. If she jumped when the door was too wide, she'd be seen. If she waited until it was too far closed, she would either be crushed or smack into the outside of the door. There was no room for error. Wiggling her behind, she prepared to pounce. She had to make it in one leap. There would be no second chance.

With the door only a foot away from sealing shut, Cali made her move. In a single bound, she propelled herself from the statue and sailed through the air. The edges of the door brushed against her fur as she flew past, landing with surprising softness on the marble floor inside. Immediately she dropped low and tucked herself behind a large trunk.

Did anyone see me? she wondered. Holding her breath, she remained perfectly still, listening for the faintest trace of human speech. Silence. She had made it without being noticed. Swiveling her head, she checked her weapon to make sure it hadn't fallen during her entrance. Thankfully, it remained secure.

Cali allowed herself to breathe again, relieved to be in position. Now it was a matter of finding the owl and hiding it from the thieves. She'd also have to find somewhere to conceal herself. Taking in her surroundings, she wasn't sure where to begin. Rows of locked metal drawers climbed all the way to the ceiling. Trunks and chests were stacked neatly along the walls.

With a sigh, Cali regretted not gaining access to the vault sooner. It was at least as large as Lionel's apartment, and she had no idea where to begin searching for the owl. *Why didn't I search the bank manager's desk for more information?* Again and again she scolded herself. There were so many roads she hadn't gone down, too many lost opportunities. Next time she vowed to be much better prepared before taking on a master criminal.

There's nothing I can do to change it now, she thought. *I'll just have to make do with what I have.* What she had was a fine set of implants, augmenting all of her natural feline abilities. Scanning the immediate area with her mechanical eye, she altered its settings in every manner possible. The owl put off no heat, nor would zooming allow her to see through the metal drawers or wooden chests. Night vision was unnecessary. The vault was illuminated with a pale yellow lamp, more than enough light for a cat.

Smelling the vault's stale air, she wondered if the owl would put off an unusual scent. It had come from a faraway island, likely a place full of spices and fruit. Maybe she could sniff it out. Trotting up and down, left and right, she sniffed in all directions. She did smell something. Pausing near a plain metal box, she ran her paws over its top. There was an unrecognizable smell to it, so she inserted her claw and practiced at the skill Emmit had shown her.

With little effort, the lock gave and the box sprang open. Cali peered inside. A tiny paper box in the shape of a lizard lay inside. Strange, unrecognizable markings of blue, red, and gold covered the paper. It had not come from this land or any she knew of. Her nose tingled at the thick layer of dust that wafted from the box. Fighting the urge to sneeze, she lifted the lizard box and sniffed it. Repulsive! It was a foul scent, one she didn't care to investigate further. Stuffing it away, she shoved the box toward the back of the vault. Whatever was inside it, she didn't want anything to do with it. It certainly wasn't the owl.

Cali took a gamble and decided not to search any of the drawers for now. She figured the owl was more likely to be in one of these chests. It needed temporary housing only here in the vault, so it was probably still in its original casing. If only she knew what the princess had used to transport it.

With vision and scent failing to lead her to the treasure, Cali decided to use the law of averages. If she searched enough of the trunks, she would eventually find what she sought. It was tedious work. Seven chests later, she still hadn't found the owl. Hissing in frustration, she swung around, working at the chests on the opposite side of the vault. At least it was a change of view.

A faint scratching sound at the vicinity of the door drew her attention away. Creeping on silent paws, she padded toward the door and listened. The pitter patter of metallic feet echoed throughout the locking mechanism. The spiderlings had reached their destination inside the lock. It wouldn't be long before they managed to open it. Cali had to work faster.

Ok, Cali, think, she said to herself. *If I were an island princess, how would I travel with a golden owl?* Answering herself, she realized it was probably within the most ornate chest in the vault. A princess would travel with only the best. Scanning the chests, her eye fell on a large trunk embellished with gold filigree. That had to be it.

Springing across the vault, Cali pounced on the opulent trunk. But then she saw something next to it. This chest was smaller, but still large enough for a cat to fit inside. The outside was solid blue, adorned with a single sapphire set in gold. *Princess Kaleyani from the Sapphire Sea,* she recalled. This had to be the one.

The scratching grew louder, prickling the hairs in Cali's ears. There was no time to lose. Inserting a mechanical claw into the lock, she twisted it with every expectation of success, but the lock didn't budge. Fear ran through the calico's heart. What if locks on the islands worked differently from the ones here? Why hadn't she searched Lisen for a key? Kicking herself would not open the box. Ignoring her own thoughts, she focused only on the lock.

"Come on," she whispered to the lock, her tongue lolling out to the side. Without her notice, her body was twisting along with her claw. Nothing worked.

Taking a step backward, Cali removed her claw. Deciding she needed a new perspective, she cocked her head to the side and studied the lock. Zooming with her mechanical eye, she saw its inner workings. To her surprise, it was similar to those Lionel had designed nearly a year ago. They were all sold to the same buyer, one Cali never laid eyes on. Could it have been the princess or her people?

It didn't matter. The spiderlings would soon break the vault lock, and Cali had to get the owl to safety. Remembering the schematics as best she could, Cali chose a new approach. The locks were tricky, and the average person would never break them. Luckily, Cali wasn't an ordinary cat, and she'd seen Lionel create the locks. Flipping upside down, Cali balanced on her head, using her tail for support. Reinserting her claw, she worked at the lock from this new angle.

Clink.

It was music to Cali's ears. She opened the lid, its hinges creaking softly. Gold glimmered before her, illuminating her tricolored fur. Diamond eyes stared into her own. If she didn't know better, she would say its expression looked grateful. The owl had no desire to be stolen by criminals.

Lifting the owl from its sanctuary, she held it toward the light. Beautiful, captivating, and surprisingly heavy. It was likely worth a fortune. Cali wouldn't have minded a few more minutes to marvel at it, but there was no time. Choosing a plain, paper crate, she concealed the owl inside. Strangely, she felt the need to apologize for placing it in such surroundings. Shaking her head, she realized it was a silly thought.

Diving inside the blue chest, she closed the lid on top of her. Now when the thieves showed up, they'd have Cali to deal with.

Chapter 13

Frozen to the windowsill, Emmit's eyes remained glued on the vault. From his position, he had an angled view of the opening. It wasn't the best vantage point, but he dared not disobey Cali. She had ordered him outside to keep watch, and that's where he intended to remain. The only exception might be for an unforeseen emergency. Fortunately, there wasn't any such thing happening right now.

He supposed she never found a way to distract the guards, since he never saw either of them leave. With little interest, he watched as the cleanup continued from the broken chandelier. It made for a rather dull afternoon. Though he couldn't see Cali, he wondered if the cat had decided to take a nap. After all, that was what cats did best. Laughing to himself, he decided that wasn't true for Cali. Yes, she enjoyed sleeping long hours, but what she did best was look out for her friends. Why else would she be in the bank right now?

Lionel certainly meant a great deal to Cali. She'd go to the ends of the earth to protect him from harm. Emmit didn't doubt she'd do the same for him. True they hadn't known each other long, but they made a good pair. After this was all over, he wondered what other adventures she might lead him on. His days as an ordinary mouse might well be over, now that he had his clockwork friend.

After a long, boring, wait, Emmit finally witnessed significant movement inside the bank. There was still no sign of the calico, but the manager had returned to his office and finalized the figures in his book. The mouse had a fairly good head for figures, so he checked the banker's math before the book was shut and stored away in the man's leather bag. When he left the office, Emmit craned his neck to keep him in his sight.

Some time passed before he witnessed Lisen and the guards entering the vault and exiting again. Cali had to make her move soon. When the bank closed, so did the vault. The mouse tried not to blink for fear of missing the feline's actions. He could not see the statue where he'd left her, but she'd have to come into view if she were walking into the vault. Assuming she hadn't already made it in somehow without his knowledge.

Continuing his vigil, he witnessed the round metal door swinging to a close, but there was no sign of the feline. Where was she? Had she been so stealthy that the mouse had completely missed seeing her? Emmit began to wonder if his attention had waned despite his best efforts to remain alert. Then suddenly, a blur of calico flew through the narrow opening an instant before the door clicked shut. The mouse nearly fell from his perch. Clutching his sides, he allowed himself a hearty laugh. A clever cat she was indeed.

As he continued to watch, the lights inside the bank dimmed. Lisen approached the window, and Emmit held his breath. Without taking notice of the mouse, the banker secured the window latch. Emmit let out a sigh of relief as the man walked away. He continued to observe as Lisen shut and locked the door to his office, leaving Emmit with a limited view of anything happening inside. From this moment on, Cali was entirely on her own. Not only was she inside the vault, but her mouse sentry could no longer see the vault door. His only way to communicate with her was through her transmitter, which conveyed little information.

The steam-powered generator behind the bank whirred to life, powering the bank's security system. It was a backup method, designed to foil burglars who knew only to disable the main wires running to the bank. But the unit was still vulnerable, so Emmit made note of its position. He would have to keep a close eye on it.

Without warning, bars descended above Emmit's head. Scrambling from his perch, he narrowly avoided being crushed from above. The window was now inaccessible to the average criminal. However, the slits between the bars would easily allow access to a clockwork spider. If only Emmit could warn the banker. With a sigh, he knew it was impossible.

Keeping low in the grass, the blue-gray mouse peeked around the corner. The entire bank staff exited at once. Tellers, guards, and the manager said their goodbyes as the door sealed shut behind them. The manager's key clicked in the lock, then in the second, and finally, in the third. Emmit doubted three locks would be enough. What he knew of Morcroft suggested the master criminal would blow up the door if he couldn't get through it easily enough.

Rather than continuing toward the street, the manager turned in Emmit's direction. The little mouse froze, terrified that he'd been spotted. Running would reveal his position, but staying put could mean certain death. His heart thundered in his chest as black leather boots closed in on him. Tucking his head beneath his arms, he awaited the crushing blow.

It never came. The banker stepped over the mouse, never looking down to acknowledge him. Emmit sank low to the ground, relief sweeping over him. Curiosity took over where the fear had been, and he decided to follow the banker to see where he was going. The man rounded the side of the bank, making his way to the rear. When he heard the generator power down, Emmit's jaw dropped open. The manager was working with Morcroft!

Or was he? The mouse tiptoed closer, scrutinizing the banker's every move. No longer did the generator puff and whir, nor was there a steady stream of vapor trailing above it. To Emmit's watchful eyes, it appeared the man had waited for his colleagues to depart and was now disabling the security backup. There was no other explanation.

Bending low, the manager inserted a small key into the unit. To Emmit's amazement, the unit powered on again, buzzing at first then steadying to a hum. Realizing his mistake, Emmit regretted his suspicion. The man hadn't been disabling the unit. He was repairing it. The loud, clunky noise it made before was a sign that it wasn't working properly. Now its soft purr was almost imperceptible. With a bit of luck, Morcroft's creations would not even know it was there.

Biting at his lip, Emmit knew that wouldn't be the case. Morcroft would have planned every single detail, leaving nothing to chance. Emmit had to be ever vigilant if he was going to be any help to Cali. Now he had to decide where to stand. He needed to see the front door, generator, and side window all at the same time. It was impossible for one mouse to do that alone.

Focusing on the setting sun, Emmit knew he had to act fast. Though Cali would want him to stay put, he knew he had to leave. There were bound to be other mice around, and he needed their help. Dashing behind the bank, he sprinted for the nearest alleyway. It wasn't far. Less than half a minute's run brought him to a series of garbage bins. A familiar squeak sounded from behind them.

"Annie?" he called to the darkened alley.

Silence answered him. The mouse had ceased her squeaking.

"Annie, is that you?" Emmit called again.

"Emmit?" the she-mouse squeaked.

"Yes," he called back. "Are you alone?" He was surprised to hear no other mice squeaking.

Instead of a verbal answer, Annie emerged from behind a bin, followed by six smaller mice. Smiling, she announced, "The girls are with me."

Emmit could have jumped for joy. "I could really use your help," he said. "All of you."

The pale gray she-mouse considered it a moment. Patting her ample stomach, she said, "I'm not sure. There's quite a stash here, you see. We haven't finished eating."

"Bring a snack with you," Emmit pleaded. "I really need the help." He and Annie had met frequently in the alleys, passing information about the best food places in Ticswyk. She owed him no favors, but he knew her to be an honest and helpful mouse. If she wouldn't help, he didn't have time to find someone else.

When Annie still didn't seem ready to travel from her feast, Emmit had another idea. "Your daughters look like the courageous sort," he said. "How would you girls like to take part in a real life adventure?"

"Can we, Mama?" four of the girls said at once. The other two looked less enthusiastic, but they didn't voice any protests.

Rolling her eyes, Annie said, "I suppose so. Grab a snack and let's see what Emmit's up to."

"It's simple," he said. "All I need you ladies to do is keep an eye out for anything strange at the bank, and squeak as loud as you can if you see something. Can you girls do that?"

The four excited mice replied, "Yes!"

One of the two reserved mice asked, "What sort of strange things are you expecting?"

"Sinister looking humans," Emmit said, "or mechanical spiders. Things like that."

Annie stopped in her tracks. "Are you putting my girls in danger?"

"Not at all," he reassured her. "Don't go anywhere near anything. Just keep a lookout from a distance and squeak. After that, I'll come running. Then you ladies can go on about your dinner with my immense gratitude."

"We will," Annie replied. With a sparkle in her eye, she added, "And you'll owe me a favor, Emmit."

Smiling, Emmit responded, "Agreed." He already knew the favor she would ask, and it would definitely involve food.

Returning to the bank, he pointed out to the girls where they could safely keep a lookout. He took a position near the window, it being the most central location. As long as Morcroft didn't surround the building, Emmit should be able to get back and forth with ease.

Waiting and listening felt like an eternity. Annie and her daughters munched happily on their dinner. The sound of their smacking set Emmit's stomach rumbling. Though he suspected it was not truly hunger but nerves affecting him. Were the spiderlings trained to attack? Did Cali have enough air in that vault? Was there a sentry lurking in there with the unsuspecting calico? He could imagine too many scenarios of things going wrong. Cali was inside and possibly already in danger. Waiting and not knowing was painful.

The sun disappeared from the sky, and Annie and her daughters had long since finished their meals. They would be hungry again soon, and Emmit didn't know how much longer he could convince them to wait. He could see the girls were growing restless, having none of the adventure they'd been promised.

As he sat quiet with his thoughts, Emmit couldn't help but think what a crazy idea this truly was. He was no detective, and Cali was not trained to subdue criminals. They should have found a way to get the police to come in their stead. But he knew Cali was probably right. The police would only laugh and think it was some sort of joke. Cats and mice didn't file police reports.

A single gas lamp lit the street corner near the bank, its warming light helping to soothe Emmit's nerves. It did little to ease his troubled mind. His thoughts continued to whirl, jumping from one doomsday scenario to the next. He began to wonder whether Morcroft was actually coming this night, or if the spiderlings had been sent for a trial run at the vault lock. When the lamp went dark, he almost didn't notice. After some time in the pitch dark, his eyes began to adjust. *What happened to the lamp?*

Instantly he knew the answer to his question. Morcroft's creatures had arrived under cover of darkness. Racing to the window, Emmit hopped up and held onto a metal bar. Inside all was dark, the red light no longer blinking on the security device in the manager's office. The main power had been cut, and it would take a few minutes for the backup generator to reactivate the security system. Emmit felt his throat tighten, his breaths coming in shallow spurts. Now was the moment for courage, and his had deserted him.

Squeak! Squeak! Two of Annie's daughters sounded the alarm, Emmit's ears twitching at the sound. Rounding the corner to the rear of the bank, the mouse was stunned. Two oversize spiders, slightly larger than Cali, were approaching the generator. Annie's girls ran from the spiders, grabbing their mother as they went.

"We're out of here," Annie said to him, gathering the rest of her daughters. "Good luck, Emmit." Speeding away, the family disappeared into the night.

Emmit was sorry to see her go, but he understood her reason. Her presence was a small comfort, but she had to keep her daughters safe. There was no way of knowing how dangerous these large spiders would be, but he was about to find out.

Keeping low in the grass to avoid detection, Emmit followed the spiders as they approached the generator. One dug furiously at the ground, the other stood idle. Were they trying to tunnel into the bank? The mouse decided not to interfere. How could he possibly disable one of the spiders, let alone two?

When the first spider had finished digging, the second reached into the ground. It pulled out a handful of wires. Now Emmit understood. They were disabling the generator, not tunneling inside. In a single swipe, the digger sliced through the wires. Sparks flew over its metal body, a charge of electricity dropping it like a stone. Relieved, Emmit now had only one spider to deal with. Maybe he could stop it from getting inside.

What happened next was nothing short of astonishing. Instead of proceeding to enter the bank, the second spider began repairs on the first. Lifting the lid of its carapace, it reached inside and fiddled with a few gears. Emmit heard clicking as one spider worked on the other. Then, it wound the mechanisms tight, and the first spider sprang back to life. *Unbelievable,*

Emmit thought. These were far more sophisticated than he'd expected them to be. That didn't bode well for Cali.

Though his knowledge of wiring was limited, Emmit knew he'd have to repair the generator. Without the security system, Cali would be entirely alone. She needed protection, and it was the only way Emmit could provide it. Despite his lack of training, he would find a way to repair the wiring, or electrocute himself in the process. For Cali's sake, he had to try. She was already risking her life, and it was time he risked his.

First, he needed to tell her they'd arrived. The transmitter lay where he'd left it beneath the window. Still keeping low, he rushed through the grass, the spiders skittering close behind. Gaining speed, they charged toward him, forcing him to roll sideways to avoid their spiky legs. Regaining his footing, he watched in horror as one of the spider's feet connected with the transmitter, sending it flying across the sidewalk. It landed hard in the street and slid to a halt.

Emmit only glanced at the spiders as they proceeded to the window and began sawing at the bars. With the grinding of metal on metal ringing in his ears, he charged toward the street. Skidding to a halt, he heard the heavy stride of a horse and the clattering of carriage wheels. Placing his paws on either side of his head, Emmit gave a soundless scream. The transmitter would be destroyed!

Placing his paws on the street, he attempted to rush out before the carriage reached it. Too late. The wheels were too close, forcing him to retreat or be squished. As the carriage sped on its way, Emmit whispered a silent prayer to the night. *Please let it be in one piece.*

Hurrying to the transmitter, Emmit couldn't believe his luck. It was scratched and dinged but otherwise unharmed. He pounced on top of it, pressing the button with all his weight. Cali would know the spiders were on their way in, and she would have time to prepare her defense. Grabbing the transmitter in his teeth, he raced back toward the generator.

Chapter 14

A single spot of keyhole-shaped light found its way into the blue chest. Cali waited inside, her mechanical eye peering out into the vault. A soft tapping echoed through the room, the sound of spiderlings working away at the locking mechanism. It was complicated. She knew it would take time for them to decode it. Morcroft might have taught them how to overcome it, but Lionel had put in so many fail-safes that even the most skilled thieves would require immense patience to open it.

Inside the owl's resting chamber there was nothing more to do but wait. Settling in, she realized she'd been waiting all day. Where was the adventure? It was about to find her. She wondered if she'd regret her decision to take on Morcroft before this night was over. It was too late to dwell on that now. She was here, and she had a job to do.

Realizing that the hour was growing late, she hoped Lionel wasn't worried. It wasn't like her to stay away for long hours, especially past dinnertime. Her rumbling stomach reminded her that she'd done just that. Salivating at the thought of tinned chicken, she licked her lips hungrily.

After an eternity crouched in the same position, she managed to stretch her legs a bit. Her arms came next, but there was still no getting comfortable inside this box. Turning in a circle, she settled herself back down and counted the clicking of the spiderlings' feet as they fiddled with the lock. When the sound stopped, she knew they'd mastered it.

The feet skittered faster now, scurrying from the lock and heading for the next task. What was it? Cali could not see, but she recognized the sound she heard.

It was metal scraping against a marble floor. The vault door was opening in the same manner it had closed. Morcroft's spiderlings had accomplished their mission. A shiver ran down her enhanced spine as she strained to hear what might happen next.

Cali's ears perked up, standing straight at attention on top of her head. Swiveling them in every direction, she searched for the spiderlings' location. Were they inside the vault? For a moment she heard nothing, and then the soft clink of metal feet. Apparently Morcroft hadn't bothered to pad the metal, knowing that no one should be inside the bank to hear them.

But Cali was there, and she wasn't going to let those little devils get away with their plan. Morcroft could find another way to line his pockets. The princess's gift would not fall into his destructive hands, and neither would the clockwork calico. Whatever it took, she would keep herself and Lionel safe from his grasp. If all went as she planned, Morcroft would find himself in a world of trouble after his heist failed. This was not only a theft, but it was also an attack on the heart of Ticswyk. Certainly this time Morcroft couldn't buy his way to freedom. It would mean jail time for sure.

At least that was Cali's hope. If Morcroft had enough troubles of his own, he'd probably give up on making Lionel's life unbearable. Chuckling at the thought, Cali knew that wasn't true. Lionel had never let Morcroft get to him. Yes, he'd been shaken up by the kidnapping, but Lionel had an indomitable spirit. He was tough and clever, and Cali was proud to call him her own. What dearer friend could a cat have?

Then her thoughts turned to Emmit. The brave little mouse was sitting vigil somewhere outside, ready to warn her at a moment's notice. What other mouse would do half as much for a cat? Cali was very lucky to have such friends.

Sudden darkness drew Cali away from her thoughts, forcing her back to reality. Peering through the keyhole, she made out the figure of the lamp. Where it had once glowed yellow was now void of power. *They've cut the electricity,* she realized. Of course they would. That would disable the security cameras, and prevent the defensive mechanism from attacking the spiderlings and whatever else Morcroft was sending.

A hint of red illuminated the darkness. Emmit had lit the beacon on the end of Cali's tail. Every muscle in her feline body tensed, her tail flicking side to side.

Hearing its thump against the inside of the chest, she forced it to keep still. This was not the time to give away her position.

Outside the vault she could hear the sound of metal being sawed. That didn't give her any sense of where the thieves would enter. It was possible they were cutting through the door, wall, ceiling, or anywhere. All she could do was stay put until they reached her, and hope that there weren't too many for her to deal with.

A loud crash echoed throughout the vault, and she suspected the entire bank as well. Whoever they were, and wherever they'd chosen to enter, it was obvious they'd succeeded. Biting at a claw, she tried to calm her nerves. Her mind wandered momentarily to Emmit, and she hoped he was someplace safe. *Stay hidden,* she projected with her mind. If only he could hear her. The last thing she wanted was for him to try to interfere on her behalf. He was a worrier, and his heart was in the right place, but he was too small and fragile to fight this battle.

Heavy footsteps plinked against the marble floor. These feet were far larger than those on the spiderlings, but they were no less metallic. Without seeing them, Cali knew what had come. Larger spiders, big enough to carry their prize away, had entered the vault. Now they were looking for the owl.

Could their eyes see through the collection of chests and metal drawers? If so, Cali's plan would fail quickly. They'd scan the area for the golden owl and be off before she could spring out of her box. If they had to check manually, she'd have time to size them up.

Focusing her mechanical eye, she hoped the spiders would come into view. Soon she got her wish. Two large spiders stepped into view. Their bodies were about the same size as hers, which was pleasing, but they stood taller, and their feet looked sharp and deadly. These had to be more sophisticated than the ones she'd already encountered. Otherwise they'd pick up the first shiny object they saw and run away with it. Better-designed enemies meant more trouble for Cali.

At least there are only two, she thought. It was only partly reassuring. One would have been the best scenario, but she'd just have to use all her wits to get through this. Beams of light shone from the brass spiders' eyes as they scanned the vault for their prize. Cali remained motionless, wondering how long it would be before they found her.

She didn't have to wait long. One spider homed in on the blue box and began to buzz. The second spider reacted by shining his eyes on the same location. With long, heavy strides they made their way through the vault and past the other chests. Ignoring everything else, they descended on the blue chest. Apparently they had known exactly what they were looking for. They hadn't needed to check any other boxes or drawers.

Cali readied herself, crouching low against the blue velvet lining. Preparing for a pounce, she hoped to disable one spider immediately, giving her the opportunity to attack the second. It was the best strategy she could think of. Being outnumbered certainly made things difficult, but she had expected no less.

Staring out the keyhole, she waited for the spiders to lift the lid. She wondered if they were capable of feeling surprise. She hoped so. The sight of her instead of the owl would send a human thief into fits. It would have been amusing if her situation weren't so serious.

As Cali maintained her attack posture, she found it strangely difficult to keep her balance. Her eyes grew wide as she realized why. The spiders had no intention of opening the chest. They were retrieving it to take back to Morcroft.

No! she thought. *I can't let them take me to his workshop.* He would dismantle her piece by piece. She had to fight now, or there wouldn't be another chance. The glint of metal visible from the keyhole suggested one spider was in front, the other in back. The chest was being carried sideways, with the opening facing between the spiders. It would have been better if she faced one of the spiders as soon as she lifted the lid. That would have given her the best chance. But it wasn't meant to be. She'd have to fight them both at once.

Before she could pounce, she remembered her homemade weapon. *Of course!* she thought. After so much time spent idle, she'd forgotten all about the explosive device she'd crafted. It was the solution to her two-spider problem. Retrieving the vial from her implants, she gripped the stopper with her paw. *Please work,* she thought. Twisting the cork, she pulled it straight out. Lifting the lid an inch, she slammed the vial into one spider.

In a flash of gray and black, the grenade exploded against the clockwork arachnid. Bolts and gears flew in every direction, shrapnel impaling the walls.

Twisted metal legs slid across the marble floor, leaving black marks as they went. Cali couldn't have been more pleased with her invention.

One down, one to go, she told herself. The first spider lost its grip on the chest, sending her tumbling to the floor. The calico landed gracefully on her feet. Now was the moment. Wiggling her haunches, she leapt for the remaining spider before it knew she was coming.

With a metallic clang, the spider crashed into the marble, weighed down by the thrashing calico. Raking with her enhanced claws, she tried to rip the automaton to pieces. No such luck. It was far too sturdy for her to shred.

Hissing, she tried to strike fear into her opponent. No good. The metal menace had no emotion. It found its way upright, standing again on eight sound legs. Cali jumped backward, her back arched, her fur bristling. Keeping her tail low, she danced around her foe, looking for any sign of an opening.

The spider's eyes gleamed with a strange, orange glow. Cali knew it was thinking. Curling its legs beneath it, it shortened its height by half. The cat thought it was a poor decision. Now they were on an even level.

To her surprise, the spider wasn't giving up. It was changing form to suit the best counterattack. Standing on half-legs, it extended the sharp metal that had previously served as its feet. Then it began to spin. Gaining momentum, it transformed itself into a whirl of blades. There was no way to attack it without being shredded.

Scanning the room, Cali searched for anything that could be used as a weapon. Her eyes stopped on the tiger statue. It was big, it was heavy, and it wouldn't back down to metal blades. It just might do the trick. Sprinting for it, she leapt over the spinning mass of metal with ease. Landing on top of the statue, she attempted to knock it off-balance.

No luck. The statue was far too heavy. There was only one chance to move it. Below her the spider continued to whirl, a cyclone of sharp metal. Losing her balance now would be like falling into a thresher. That was a ride she didn't intend to take.

Placing herself between the statue and the wall, she shoved with all her might. Pushing her enhanced legs to their limit, she barely managed to wiggle the statue. Pausing for a breath, she tried a second time. Heaving her body against the marble, she managed to tip it just enough to unbalance it. In a thunderous crash, it slammed against the floor, taking out three of the spider's legs. It spun sideways, its balance obliterated by the statue's weight. It could no longer maintain the cyclone.

The spider wasn't giving up just yet. As she watched, it transformed itself again, shifting its good legs to compensate for the damaged ones. Cali groaned in frustration. What would it take to disable this thing? There was no time to think. The spider extended a sharpened leg, intending to run the cat through. She rolled to one side, narrowly avoiding the piercing blade.

Racing to the far end of the bank, Cali looked everywhere for another weapon. She came up empty. Focusing on the manager's door, she was both surprised and relieved to see it wide open. Dashing inside, she slammed the door behind her. Turning to secure the latch, she realized it was broken. This was how the spiders had come in. Behind her the window stood open. A large, rectangular section had been sliced from the metal bars that were intended to prevent a burglary. Some good they had done.

The desk was her only option now. Still in one piece, it was heavy enough to barricade the door while she formulated a new plan. As she braced herself against the wall and prepared to shove the desk, a glint in one partially opened drawer caught her eye. A pistol! Opening the drawer, she retrieved the weapon.

Despite her lack of firearms training, Cali knew a few things. If it was loaded, then pulling the trigger might create a similar effect to her homemade explosive. There was one sure way to find out. Pulling open the door, she came face to face with the spider. Clenching the pistol in her teeth, she aimed for the spider's carapace. With one enhanced claw, she pulled the trigger.

A deafening boom erupted from the pistol, striking the arachnid square in its metal head. Cali recoiled, her ears ringing and teeth chattering. The pistol dropped to the ground. She waited a moment for the smoke to clear before determining her enemy's fate. Straight ahead, she spotted the automaton. It shook itself, all of its legs trembling momentarily. Then it continued forward, charging at the feline.

Cali couldn't believe it. A wide, round hole punctured the spider, leaving a trail all the way through its carapace. Light could be seen from the other side, and the sound of its gears clicked louder than before. Despite its ragged appearance, the spider had survived her attack.

Leaping high, Cali avoided the charging sentry and launched herself back into the bank's main chamber. It was possible many weapons awaited in the vault, but finding them would take too long. The spider was already on her, skittering on sharpened feet, one leg slicing at the air.

With no weapons at hand, Cali improvised. A bowl of hard candy on a nearby desk proved itself quite heavy. She heaved it at the oncoming spider, knocking it off-balance. As it tried to regain its footing, it slipped on bits of spilled candy.

Cali was surprised to discover that candy worked better than a pistol. But there was no time to contemplate such matters. She had to keep moving and keep fighting. As a last resort, she would retrieve the owl and use it as a hammer. It was far heavier than the spider, but it could be damaged in the process. She didn't know what else to do. With the spider on her again, she had to make another jump, flinging herself across the room. Her mind raced along with her legs, her heart pounding in her ears. Despite her enhancements, she was still a creature of flesh and blood. Her body would give out with exhaustion long before her clockwork opponent's. She had to find a way to disable it.

Chapter 15

Emmit stopped short of reaching for the wires, his

paws poised inches above them. There was no sign of electricity running through them, but he preferred to be cautious. Touching a live wire could be the last thing he ever did. An accommodating leaf nearby was the solution to his problem. Within the cupped leaf was a small amount of water, collected from recent rain. Standing clear, the mouse tossed the water onto the wires and jumped away. No sparks.

Double checking the generator, he made sure the switch was set to the off position. He didn't want it kicking on and delivering him a nasty shock. After a few deep breaths, he was ready to begin working. Reaching into the hole dug by the spiders, he lifted the frayed wire's end. Wrapped inside a casing that appeared to be rubber were several copper wires.

It was the first time Emmit had ever handled such a thing. His mother had warned him never to chew through these cables because they were dangerous. He'd always heeded her advice. Now here he was trying to *unchew* the wire. Thankfully his mother wasn't watching him now.

Inspecting the wires, he realized it wasn't all that complicated. If he attached the copper bits together, the electricity would probably flow as it had before. The only problem was matching the correct wire to its other half. Or did that matter? He couldn't answer that question.

Studying each wire, he determined which cut ends matched, the two fitting together like a puzzle piece. Twisting those wires together, he formed a continuous cable for the current to flow through. The work was tedious but not overly difficult. It would take time.

Emmit's tiny paws flew as he continued to pull and twist at the wires. His paw pads grew sore, his joints aching, but still he continued. He didn't dare try twisting the wires with his mouth. His mother's warning rang loud in his ears, despite the lack of power to the wires.

A loud boom inside the bank startled the mouse, who dropped the wires to the ground. Was Cali all right? Had the spiders just blown up the door to the vault? Returning to his work, his paws flew feverishly over the wires. Ignoring his discomfort, he refused to slow down. Cali was in danger, more than he'd anticipated. If he could get the security system up and running, it would help her. An alarm would definitely sound when it detected movement. There was a chance it would frighten the intruders away, but he doubted it. Morcroft would have prepared them for that scenario. But the police would definitely respond to the alarm, and they'd stop the spiders. He only hoped that Cali lasted that long.

Again and again he reminded himself what a clever cat she was. With all of her enhancements, she was strong enough, and fast enough, to keep herself out of harm's way. Yes, he was certain the sound he'd heard was a sign that she was winning. He refused to believe any different.

Finally all the wires were connected and there was only one thing left to do. Hopping on top of the generator, he flipped the switch. A spark of electricity shot from the cord, and Emmit shielded his eyes from the light. A brief silence suggested he'd failed in his attempt to repair the damage, but when the generator began to buzz, he knew he'd succeeded.

Turning a backflip, he celebrated this small victory. The buzzing grew louder, and the entire system began to vibrate. Emmit hopped down and stood clear. Steam bellowed from the exhaust port on the generator's back end as it whirred itself to full power.

Dashing to the window, Emmit realized that the security bars had been cut. This was where the spiders had entered while he'd been occupied elsewhere. The manager's door stood open, and the little mouse could see inside the bank. The vault door was open, but he saw no sign of Cali.

Knowing Cali wouldn't want him to come after her didn't matter anymore. He had to go in. She might need his help, and there was nothing else to do outside. Diving through the window, he crept on silent paws to the doorway. A squeak of surprise sounded from his throat as he laid eyes on the scene before him.

Out of the security camera's sight, Cali rode on the back of a spider. Bits of mangled metal strewn around the bank suggested she'd already dispatched one. Emmit smiled to himself, proud of his friend's accomplishment. Too small to set off the camera himself, he'd be able to let Cali know that they were armed. The rest would be up to her.

Holding on tight, Cali managed to keep herself on top of the spider as it ran in circles, trying to shake her loose. She'd managed to bend one of its legs, forcing it to walk with a limp. It was slowed but not fully impaired. She needed a new plan and quick.

Holding on with enhanced hind legs, she swung her paws under the spider's belly. Raking with her metallic claws, she managed to pull open a hatch inside it. Was this where its power source was housed? It was certainly worth finding out. Righting herself, she caught a quick breath before attempting another attack. To her surprise, the spider headed straight for the vault door, careening toward it with its head low.

It's trying to crush me! Thinking quick, she somersaulted off the spider's head, landing softly on her feet. The arachnid tried to stop, but slid into the door, denting its already damaged carapace. Cali wanted to laugh, but there was no time. She had to get to its belly.

A loud squeak from Lisen's doorway drew her attention. There stood Emmit, waving his paws and screaming at the top of his lungs. Cali swallowed her anger. He was not supposed to be here. A quick sprint across the room brought her to his side.

"What is it?" she shouted.

"The security system is armed," he told her. "Use it!"

Glancing up at the camera, Cali saw the red light blinking. "Good work," she said to Emmit as she galloped away.

Shaking off its injury, the clockwork spider righted itself and came after her again. Cali positioned herself in the camera's view, and stood on her hind legs. A piercing alarm echoed through the bank, the blinking red light changing to a steady, menacing eye.

Silently counting down in her head, Cali waited for the right moment. The spider crept closer, closer, and then it was right where she wanted it. Dropping on all fours, she swept a leg, tripping the spider and sending it skittering into the camera's view. Cali jumped clear, a crackling hiss resonating in her ears. Just the sound she was expecting.

Grabbing Emmit and clutching him close, she ducked inside the manager's office. With the spider still off-balance, it had nowhere to run. A bolt of electricity flew from the camera's red eye, surging through the metallic monster. It shuttered and quaked before collapsing to the floor in a heap of charred metal.

"Woohoo!" cried Emmit, leaping into the air.

Cali didn't bother to hide her delight. She patted her mouse friend on the back. "I couldn't have done it without you," she said.

Emmit beamed with pride. "I do what I can," he said. "We'd better get out of here before the police show up." The alarm still sounded, and soon there'd be a crowd forming. It would be best if they weren't seen.

"There's one more thing I have to do," Cali said.

Whatever it was, Emmit hoped it wouldn't take long.

Returning to the scene of the crime, Cali searched the debris. "We need one or two of those gears," she said.

"What gears?" Emmit asked.

"The ones with Morcroft's mark on them," she responded. "They're his own make, and they'll prove he was behind this." Her mechanical eye examined every scrap of metal on the floor. "Like this!" she shouted, diving for a gear. Lifting it with her paw, she said, "If you find another, put it with this one." Carefully laying it on top of the defunct automaton, she raced back into the vault.

"Where are you going?" Emmit called after her.

"To get the owl," she replied. Gently lifting it from its hiding place, she caressed it with her paw. It was as beautiful as she remembered. The night's strange events hadn't affected it at all. Proud that the prized gift had not been damaged, she returned to the central chamber and placed it inside the blue chest. Closing the lid on top of it, she bid the item farewell.

"I found another gear," Emmit said, placing it next to the first. "Now can we get out of here?"

Nodding, Cali led him back to the office and lifted him to the windowsill. A crowd had indeed gathered out front, citizens in their nightclothes whispering and pointing. A group of police shoved their way through the crowd, approaching the bank's front entrance.

Cali and Emmit disappeared into the night, leaving the police to their work. There was no denying who had committed the crime. Such an insult to Ticswyk would not go unanswered. Now it was up to the courts to take on the Guilds and see that Morcroft faced justice. There was nothing more the cat-and-mouse team could do.

* * * * *

"Lionel?" Florence called through the door. "Lionel, wake up. You have to see this!"

Cali stretched at the foot of the bed, waiting for Lionel to don his robe and slippers. When he was ready, she hopped from the bed and followed him to the door.

Yawning, he reached for the handle and opened it. "Morning, Flo," he said. Shuffling toward his chair, he plopped down heavily. It was an hour earlier than his normal waking time.

Florence hurried after him and handed him the newspaper. "Morcroft's been arrested," she announced.

Lionel scratched the top of his head. "What for?"

"He tried to steal the golden owl," she told him. "It's all there in the article."

Lionel didn't have his glasses, so he squinted at the photo in the paper. Morcroft appeared in handcuffs, a police officer pointing to a prisoner's carriage. Shaking his head, Lionel could hardly believe his eyes. "So that's what he wanted my help with," he commented. Patting his lap he invited Cali to join him in his chair. She curled up on his lap and purred. "Good thing Cali rescued me from his grasp," he said. "Otherwise, I could be cuffed right next to him."

"No," Florence said. "You never would have given in. I know you too well."

The Master Tinker gave no argument. She was right, as usual. He wouldn't have worked on any project for Morcroft, no matter the consequences. "I wonder what he wanted with that owl."

"Probably to melt it down," she said. "You know how Morcroft is. He commits crimes solely to prove that he can. He thinks he's invincible."

"True," Lionel responded.

"Well this time someone did catch him," Florence said. "The security cameras were damaged, so there's no photograph of whoever was there, but there were two mechanical spiders, only one of which was damaged by the security system. The other was blown to bits by some other means."

"Hmm," Lionel replied, his eyebrows raised high. It was good to hear that someone was looking out for the community and wasn't afraid to stand up to Morcroft. "It's probably best whoever it was remains anonymous," he said. "Morcroft and the Guilds will be looking for revenge. They won't like it one bit that someone interfered." He stroked Cali's fur casually, unaware of her part in the foiled heist.

"There was damage outside too," Florence went on. "Apparently the thieves cut the wires to the backup generator. Someone repaired them."

"That's dangerous work," Lionel commented.

"Indeed," she replied. "I'm going to ask Mr. Lisen to show me everything later today."

Laughing, Lionel replied, "I'm sure he'll be happy to do so." He knew she grew fonder of the bank manager by the day. Luckily for him the owl hadn't been stolen. It probably would have cost him his career. Though he wasn't at fault, the citizens would be outraged. They would say he hadn't done enough to protect the valuable item. Whoever had foiled the robbery, Lisen owed that person a debt of gratitude. "I expect your banker will offer a reward to the person responsible for saving the owl."

"Perhaps, but there's no way to prove who it was," she replied. "Everyone would try to take the credit in order to claim the reward."

"You're right," Lionel said. *As usual,* he added silently. He'd heard enough about golden owls and master criminals. It was time for breakfast. "Did you bring any pastries?" he asked.

She handed him a small brown bag full of savory sweets. Lionel's eyes gleamed as he accepted the gift.

Cali's ears perked up, her nose wiggling at the familiar scent. One of the pastries was definitely filled with cream cheese, a favorite of hers, and she suspected of Emmit's as well. The clockwork calico stifled a laugh. It looked like the cat-and-mouse pair would get a reward for saving the owl after all.

About the Author

Lana Axe lives in the Missouri countryside surrounded by dogs, cats, birds, and reptiles. She spends most of her free time daydreaming about elves, magic, and faraway lands.

For more information, please visit: lana-axe.com.

15531862R00131

Made in the USA
Lexington, KY
13 November 2018